Breathe the Sky

A NOVEL
Inspired by the Life of Amelia Earhart

CHANDRA PRASAD

Wyatt-MacKenzie Publishing, Inc.

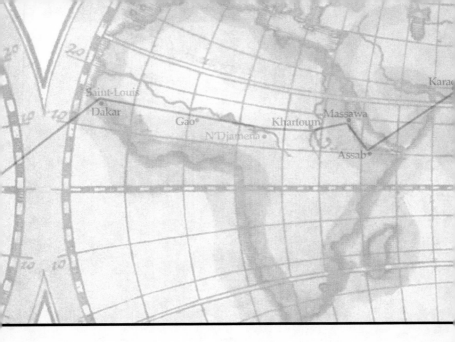

To Niki

* * *

Breathe the Sky by Chandra Prasad

F I R S T   E D I T I O N
ISBN: 978-1-932279-39-9
Library of Congress Control Number: 2009930482

Cover photo provided courtesy of Purdue University, from Purdue University Libraries'
The George Palmer Putnam Collection of Amelia Earhart Papers.

While many of the incidents and characters here have some basis in the life and times of
Amelia Earhart, *Breathe the Sky* is a work of fiction and should be read solely as thus.

Wyatt-MacKenzie Publishing, Inc.
15115 Highway 36, Deadwood, Oregon 97430
541-964-3314 * www.wymacpublishing.com

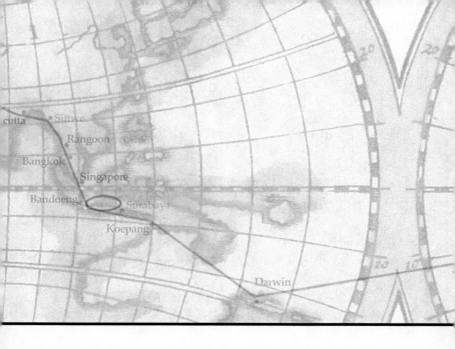

Contents

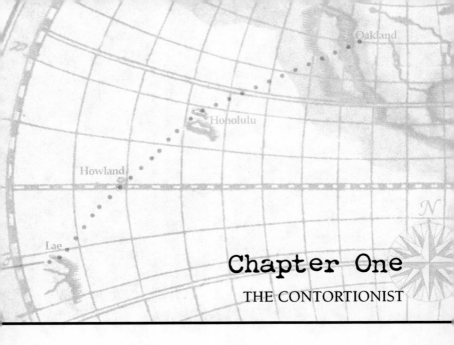

Chapter One

THE CONTORTIONIST

IT STARTED, OFFICIALLY, WITH THE NOTE. IN HER MIND it started with the little torn scrap he passed in the minutes before that first doomed leg of her flight around the world. He passed it from the back of the plane to the front, on the end of the bamboo fishing pole: their modest communication system.

As she took the note, the metal clip at the end of the pole gave a surprisingly ferocious squeak. Like a Pavlovian dog, she heard the sound as a harbinger of something palatable. Not that it had been that way at first. She'd always detested even the slightest distraction while flying. Some pilots liked to hum, listen to a loudly ticking watch, snap their chewing gum, or sing. A.E. found all of these inappropriate, somehow, as if any earthly sound disrupted the purity of being in the air. But now, well, when the clip squeaked, it squeaked. She didn't mind so much.

Good luck, my brave girl, the note read.

It was the "my" that made her think. "My": a surprisingly possessive word choice. She smiled, lips shut. She'd trained herself to smile this way. No teeth, better for the photographs, G.P. had told her.

"Gives you an unreachable, magisterial look, like a bygone queen."

This declaration struck her as funny in the torpid heat of the cockpit, where stains were already blooming at her armpits, where gasoline, grease, and sea smells commingled not entirely sociably.

My brave girl.

G.P. wouldn't like that, she decided, folding the note into a tight, perfect square and tucking it into one of the front pockets of her jumpsuit, along with the other mementoes she was carrying: the silver pilot's wings of the U.S. Air Service and a letter from a young fan in Connecticut named Cecilia DeRisio. Most prized, perhaps, was a list of intrepid women A.E. had collected through the years: a pistol shot champion out of Texas named Grace, the first woman in India to be admitted to the bar, Oklahoma's only female bank president, the United States Civil Service Commissioner, who also called herself a home-maker, and so on, all the pioneering women she'd heard and read about, their names recorded in tiny cramped scrawl, front and back.

As for Fred's note, well, she might sneak it out and read it again hours from now, if the sky were clear, if she could afford to look askance.

Outside, the crowd that had gathered before dawn was cheering raucously. Their voices drowned by the whir of machinery, the people looked like hapless mimes. She ignored the attention. She didn't favor crowds, and especially reporters, when starting a high-risk venture. Only when finishing it.

On the 3000-foot hard surface runway of Luke Field, she blinked through the windshield of the cockpit. An earlier rain had left a million liquidy finger-streaks. The air still hung heavily with condensation. At her request, the floodlights came to life, seeming to illuminate more shadows than they vanquished. The gothic contours of the landscape jarred her. She gave the engineers another signal and the lights went off. Her pupils minimized as the terrain resettled into normalcy, the military shacks and makeshift buildings and tanks in the immediate distance no longer hulking nascent monsters, and farther away, the mountains now serene, haloed in soft white mist. She started both engines. The plane's wheel chocks were hauled away. A firm-postured lieutenant issued the all-clear signal and she guided her Lockheed Vega to the end of the runway. Scores of flashlights cut through the early morning light. Little dancing glints, like fireflies, she thought. At the line on the ground A.E. braked, turned the engines to idle, rechecked the pressure and temperature gauges. Normal. Everything normal. The small army of engineers on base had inspected every inch of the Lockheed in the last twenty-four hours, and they'd addressed all problems, including a deposit of sediment in the fuel tank. Her confidence was bolstered by their thoroughness, and also by her crew. Manning and her note-giver, Noonan, sat in the navigator's compartment. They were two of the most knowledgeable, reliable comrades a pilot could have, surely. She'd expressed this exact sentiment to G.P., although he hadn't looked convinced.

The note was in a far corner of her mind as she let go the brakes and advanced the throttles. Eagerly, the plane pushed forward. A.E. held steady the control yoke. Her feet skipped carefully on the rudder pedals. She took several deep breaths, the brusque tang of pineapple juice drunk hours ago still on her tongue. In her peripheral vision the dozens of young officers who had helped her prepare for this moment were frozen in proud, anxious anticipation; the admirers jostling and surging at the barrier tape.

The plane, her beloved pet—really, her only true love—at first showed no distress. It started to drift off-center so slowly A.E. didn't notice until the straight line on the runway began angling to the right. Another deep breath. She tried to compensate by pushing the left rudder pedal, a little, at first, then as far as it would go. The suspicion that something wasn't right iced into fact. She felt this with the cool-headedness of a seasoned aviatrix, but also with the primal dread of a child. She wondered what the inspectors could have missed, what she could have missed too. The wings seemed to rock, and now maybe she had overcompensated, for the whole ship veered jerkily to the left. She was no longer working with her Lockheed, but separate from it: it had asserted its power and detached from her, the invisible umbilical cord that united them snapping swiftly and unpredictably, as was its right. Only the foolish pilot believed too strongly in his own command.

Now the leftward tilt had become a horrible urgent detour. The plane gained panicked speed as it wobbled, the controls trembling in her hands, under her feet. In her bones it seemed. The wings, like a trapped bird's, flailed haplessly. The landing gear collapsed. The craft fell forward on its belly, painfully, grinding, screaming, shouting against the ground, sparks lighting up the air like some hokey, small-town fireworks show. Her lips pressed tensely. Hysterics weren't her nature. She'd never in her life screamed. It was just another stereotypically feminine habit she wasn't prone to; it was, in fact, one she detested and would have consciously avoided anyway. The plane continued its wild, belly-first run. Skidding, sliding, a protesting land-bound beast, until, after what seemed like an eternity, it stopped.

She thought, first, am I dead? The stench of something oily and charred burned her nostrils, so that she wasn't quite sure if she were in hell. Second, she wondered, if not in hell, would she die now? After all this abuse, the fuselage was bound to blow. Sitting in the plane was like taking a grenade, pulling its stem, and holding it against her breast.

Swiftly, calmly, she opened the overhead hatch. She

climbed out of her seat, realizing she needed to vomit. But not here, she resolved. Not in front of anyone. She would not heap personal embarrassment onto an already spectacular failure.

* * *

Noonan came away with nothing but a scraped elbow. A.E. claimed a bruised ego. It was further assaulted when Noonan told her that Manning considered the incident her fault.

"That's ridiculous. It was the right shock absorber, obviously."

Noonan took a hard slug of whiskey. He smiled obliquely. His eyes, A.E. thought, were about to blur into oblivion. She'd seen this dress rehearsal before. All of a sudden her little crush seemed ridiculous, even masochistic.

"Sweetheart, it might just be the two of us next time," he told her.

"That's fine with me."

"You're not angry?" He was teasing, but taunting too.

"Angry, no. Annoyed, yes."

Noonan's gaze trailed to the empty glass. When he looked at her again she couldn't deny that a part of him was dead sober.

"Well cheer up, kitty-cat. You've still got eight lives left."

* * *

She'd wanted to resume immediately. Not in a month, or a week, but tomorrow, even today. Right this damn second, she thought, a fury rising in her. She had recently given another speech, this one to alumni at Purdue University, and she'd aced it. It had been a perfectly controlled, perfectly apt address, full of hope and vigor, her voice certain and resolute, and yet she'd felt doubt filling many of the eyes on her. Had it been real, she wondered, or had she simply seen her own fear reflected in their eyes? Either way it was ridiculous that she still needed to prove herself, even after braving the Atlantic alone, earning a Distinguished Flying Cross for heroism, and being named one of the world's most influential women. The Army's 381st Aero Squadron had made her an honorary major. She was one of the first five women in history to earn a transport license. She'd been received by both the Pope and Mussolini, courted for autographs by Marlene Dietrich, Mary Pickford, Bing Crosby, and Gary Cooper. The Fashion Designers of America loved her and Vogue called her "The First Lady of the Sky." And still she was wracked by a secret inadequacy. Almost 40 now, still she felt the wild girlish nag to push higher than they thought she could, to achieve more, to win, to fight, so that they—whoever *they* were—couldn't deny her.

Leave 'em slack-jawed with awe, as G.P. had said.

She looked at her breakfast: toast with strawberry jam spread meticulously to the edges. Her bite marks were tiny, neat. Her back against the chair was braced.

G.P. appeared and snatched the toast from her plate, took a mouthful and then set it down again. Affectionately, he patted her head. He was handling the reporters on the back end, as usual. He'd already dashed off a press release and made the right phone calls, negating her culpability and repeating the phrase "mechanical failure" until it sounded like the truth. He'd told her to write about the crash from her perspective. They'd get it published in the *Tribune*, tomorrow if she could finish a draft by four p.m., guaranteed.

"We've got it all under control," he told her.

She smiled wryly. "I'm going to try again, so don't try to talk me out of it. As soon as the plane is ready, I'm off."

"You're off," he echoed. His easy consent made her nervous.

"You're not going to try to talk me out of it?"

"Why should I? It didn't work before."

He rubbed her shoulders and kissed her on the forehead. The frame of his eyeglasses grazed her cheek.

A.E. picked up the plate of toast and handed it to her husband. An image of Noonan, of the note, flashed briefly in her memory. But she didn't feel guilty, guilt being another feminine tendency she did her best to avoid.

★ ★ ★

The short lull Amelia was hoping for would turn into a long drudgery. The necessary repairs were more extensive than she'd thought. The Lockheed needed to be rehauled, refitted, refurbished, essentially reincarnated. Such a transformation, A.E. knew, would take more than elaborate stratagems. It would require cash. Fortunately, G.P. was forging ahead with his usual bravado, committing her to radio interviews, product advertisements, social calls with current financiers, and parties with prospective ones. She was used to the rigmarole. Over the years she'd seen her name attached to a luggage line, fur-lined flying suits, U.S. postal stamps, Bausch and Lomb sunglasses, Beech Nut foods, Kodak Cameras, and any of a number of humbler endorsements she'd rather not recall. G.P. had her flitting around Hollywood, too. She'd told him sternly that she had no desire to be in a film, even if the money was good. But he shopped around her story anyhow. For one lucky actress it would be the role of a lifetime, he'd said.

In between everything else there were the speeches, and boy were there a lot of them, all over the country, so that if she weren't standing behind a podium or college lectern, she was flitting from city to city in the Electra or in her big rattling Franklin sedan. When she ought to have been resting, she churned out newspaper editorials, letters of reference, and recruiting materials for the Ninety-Nines, the aviation organization created a few years ago by 99 female pilots, including herself. She headlined rallies to promote the Democratic party, women's rights, and the expansion of commercial aviation. She had a pen with her at all times, and wasn't adverse to scribbling on fliers, paper napkins, even on her own hand. Most nights her typewriter droned on well past midnight.

It was a relentless game, and sometimes she resisted it. To escape she made impromptu visits to schools and orphanages. The sight of children could always put things in perspective. The excitement of young voices invigorated. She'd realize, immediately, how lucky she was, how everything she had was a matter of chance. She wondered, of these children, which would be blessed by greater opportunity. Little girls tugged at her hands; little boys clung to her shirttails. She kept a stock of presents in the back of the Franklin: a doll with yellow yarn hair, a velvet pillow, an embroidered quilt square—special keepsakes she hoped would soothe and mother after she'd gone.

When she'd worn herself into utter disrepair, too wrecked even to drive, she'd pull over. Head on the steering wheel, she'd snooze. She would doze right there on the shoulder of the road, where anyone could find her. And when she'd truly done herself in, when there was nothing else to give, there were the episodes in the hospital, for the sinus infections that never quite went away.

More than her lifestyle, the masquerade exhausted her. Everyone thought she and G.P. were fabulously wealthy. For god's sake, her own sister expected handouts. Muriel assumed A.E.'s dresser drawers were lined with gold foil. Admittedly, she and G.P. projected a gilt image. Her husband came from old money. His grandfather had built a publishing behemoth: G.P. Putnam's Sons, whose success hadn't waned since its founding, fifty years ago.

A.E. herself knew about old money: the lacquered look of

it, the jealousy it could kindle. If you came from old money, it almost didn't matter if you ran out. You carried the essence of it with you. The financial fate of her own parents had veered like the Franklin's speedometer, but she'd always felt more in line with the gentry. Always she'd exuded a well-to-do evenness. The scarves around her neck were of the finest Italian silk and if she tied them a certain way, there was no way to see the iron burns, the long-set stains.

Thus, it seemed reasonable, even right, to spend hundreds on planes and equipment, vacations, nice dinners, French champagne, assistants, maids and groundskeepers, and gifts for their richer friends. Appearances needed to be made. Appearances needed to be kept up. Her wardrobe was an expensive, cinematic study in contrasts: well-tailored trousers, greasy coveralls, blouses with sleeves rolled up just so, an oil rag or bandanna draped precisely from a pocket. After buying a new leather coat, she'd sleep in it till it looked lived-in. She'd spatter it tactically with oil and brush the cuffs with engine grease. When the reporters latched onto her "tousled hair," she relied on the curling iron as much as the wind. The first thing she did after landing was powder her nose.

She didn't fault herself for cultivating her image. Powerful men had done it since time immemorial. Practicality, as much as vanity, inspired her. In a white-gloved way, she and her husband lived hand-to-mouth. There were always bills waiting worrisomely on the kitchen table, and she paid for half. This was not something she and G.P. discussed. This was how it was.

* * *

Time passed, days into weeks, weeks into months, and now the trade winds had changed. A.E. would have to circumnavigate the world in the opposite direction, leaving from Florida and flying east. Reversing course required new data of every kind. A.E. was most concerned with having accurate maps. Mountains, jungles, valleys, lakes: these were not static entities. They revised themselves when approached from different directions. She didn't have time to comb for information again, to start planning anew. And yet she'd be daft to rely on hastily assembled directives. On navigational matters, she must trust Noonan completely.

She thought about postponing the trip until next year, so that she could follow the original route. This was her most logical option. There was simply too much commotion in her head right now, with her father's passing and the bad press from the Hawaii flap. It would be simpler, really, to wait. Yet she'd staked her legacy on this trip. She'd invested everything: her money, the whole of her happiness. She didn't want to add extra months to the mortgage if she didn't have to.

No, she would press on as soon as possible, and use the reverse route. The tour promised to be brutal, and the last legs would be hair-raising. In particular, she was concerned about the penultimate flight, from New Guinea to Howland Island. Howland was nothing more than a random dot in the middle of the South Pacific. It measured two miles by less than one. Her friend, Jackie Cochran, likened its size to the Cleveland airport. Bad weather could easily obscure it from view. A tiny navigational error could throw her into a void of ocean. Even more upsetting, the flight to Howland was lengthy: 18 hours, under optimal conditions. This was almost the extent of her fuel capacity. The margin for error was slim indeed, too slim for comfort. In aviation things went wrong all the time. She had to expect they *would* go wrong.

"I'm working out the logistics," Putnam told her one evening. He could read the barometer of her anxiety with superb accuracy.

"Tapping the usual resources?"

"All of them."

The troops needed to be rallied again: the Navy, Coast Guard, Departments of Interior and State, international agents, even the President and Eleanor. All must be stroked, cajoled, and reeducated. As before, it would be a complicated process requiring decisiveness and diplomacy, brass knuckles and kid gloves. G.P. wasn't the best person for the job. But truth be told, she didn't want it either.

*　*　*

The repeating nightmare was getting the better of her. She yearned for any palliative. Though she normally avoided medication, she acquiesced this once. Finding a spare razorblade in the medicine cabinet, she bisected one of the salmon-colored pills Doctor Brannigan had prescribed, swallowing half with a sip of seltzer water. She lay down for a few minutes, a sweet, welcome haziness overtaking her.

The phone rang. It was her mother.

In her quiet, exasperatingly passive way, Amy explained how the gaberdine gaucho-style trousers A.E. had sent her were beautiful and unusual, but a little baggy. They weren't becoming at all. Amy felt—how could she put it—like a hobo.

"But I don't mean to complain," she added.

Always with her mother, there was this waltz.

"I'll buy you a new pair," A.E. said groggily. "One size down."

"Oh no, that's too much."

"It's no trouble."

"Are you sure?"

"Yes, Mother."

"Because I don't want to inconvenience you."

"It's no trouble."

"Oh, thank you. Thank you. How lovely, dear. You know, your sister admired those pants so."

A.E. paused. "All right, I'll try to get Pidge a pair too," she said, irritable now.

"You sound tired, dear."

"I haven't gotten much sleep lately."

"You've been doing too much. Take a break. Don't feel like you have to entertain me, Amelia. I have bread dough all over my hands, anyhow. Boy, am I making a mess."

Something lodged in A.E.'s throat, and she thought, abruptly, that she would like very much to hug her mother right now, to touch the tidy, comforting upsweep of her hair.

"Good-bye," A.E. said, unable to chase the petulance from her voice.

"Good-bye. I hope you sleep. I love you."

And now, a weary daughter wondered why it was so much easier to be kind and affectionate in letters. She asked herself, just when exactly, she had become the caretaker, her mother the dependent.

* * *

Though she suppressed her jitters, she couldn't eliminate them. Her appetite snapped on and off. Her tanned skin turned splotchy, temperamental, oily along the patrician forehead. She napped now, frequently, whereas before she'd rather have taken a walk, chatted with friends, listened to music, or gone out for a drive. The naps didn't alleviate a deeper weariness, though. Not one to remember her dreams, she lately awoke in acute panics, sweat drenching her clothes, the same nightmare repeating itself. Noonan, only grayer, older—or no, she was mistaken, it was her father—wreaking of alcohol, stinking of it through his suit, his very pores, and still she, a child, clung trustingly to his hand, loved him unquestioningly, as he guided her through a crowd, then bent down to pick her up and carry her on his shoulders. She sat there, hands poised on his head for balance, her own head tilted back. It was the air show she'd seen on Christmas Day in 1920: the Aeronautical Club of Southern California's Winter Air Tournament. In real life, she'd been 23 years old. But in the foggy dreamscape she looked with a child's wonder at the exquisitely furtive daredevil planes. They caroused and converged, divorced, converged again. She didn't blink during the finale, the grand dive, six tin noses screeching toward the ground for greater drama, bodies squeezed close, wing to wing. In her nightmare the planes didn't curb up. Like dizzy flies kept in an upside-down Mason jar, they wobbled in their last moments of life. Then one by one they fell aground, carving great fiery holes. At the same time, her father casually threw her from his shoulders. She became an orphan to the air.

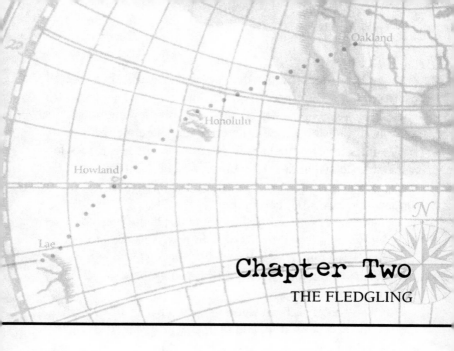

Chapter Two
THE FLEDGLING

IT HAD BEEN MAY 1903, THE BEGINNING OF A NEW CENTURY. A.E. felt the promise of this, somehow. She was six years old, watching intently as her father held his wingtip shoes to his face, exhaled on their surfaces, and buffed away the smudges of moisture with a rag. Amy was worried, but tried to keep her anxiety contained in the kitchen. An occasional pained moan accompanied her footsteps on the floorboards. While she returned dishes to the cupboard with a clatter, a tottering Muriel played with her dolls.

A.E. stared at Edwin in the shabby alcove with its awful burgundy wallpaper. Even against this backdrop, she was quite sure there had never been a more handsome man than her father. His hair was a meticulously oiled, gleaming wave cresting from his forehead. His shoes, once returned to his feet, were flossy-bright. The shine at each polar end made his whole body glow.

He called out to Amy, who ventured in. Her eyes darted from side to side, never seeming to settle on Edwin. A.E.

listened very carefully to what her father said. These were words she'd heard before; Edwin had repeated them with varying levels of enthusiasm during the past few months. He was about to travel to Washington, D.C. There, he would file a patent for a device he had invented. It had something to do with railroad signal flags. A wonder no one has thought of it yet, her father said. The trip would be expensive, and A.E. understood this upset her mother.

"But are you one hundred percent sure?" she pressed.

"How many times must I explain this? You need to put a little gas in the tank to get the vehicle moving."

"I just want you to be *sure*. This isn't a game we're playing. Papa has warned you about. . ."

Edwin shook his head vigorously. His cheeks, fine chiseled ridges, flushed. Amy stopped talking.

"I've told you how I've thought this through. I've thought it through a hundred ways till Sunday. This is something the railroad industry needs. They'll buy it!"

His voice was getting louder. It tended to do this at night. A.E.'s father often came home from work restless, irritable with ideas no one wanted to hear, least of all Amy.

When he left to begin the long drive east, A.E. smiled after him. She was proud of the way he looked as he shut the door: unstoppable. He wasn't always like this. Normally the topic of Amy's father impaired him. When the family visited her grandparents' house, Edwin turned into a little boy. He forgot things he'd learned decades ago: not to slouch, to start with the outside utensils and work in, to look a man in the eye when speaking. Her father shrunk in the brocade armchairs. His feet contracted upon the leather ottomans. His head fell short of all headrests. When Grandpa Otis asked him a question, his voice rose to a high, pubescent octave. The arresting contour of his jaw turned mushy. His eyes closed intermittently, giving him a sleepy, almost idiotic air.

There were also changes A.E. didn't notice, like the distortion Edwin felt keenly when near his father-in-law. Edwin heard Judge Otis's voice not as a voice, but as noise, a bothersome sound stationed somewhere between resignation and bitter intolerance. In the judge's presence, Edwin dragged along the pitiable poverty of his childhood. He had shoes now, but his feet still felt naked and cold. He was married, yet it was as though he were stuck back in his precarious, five-year engagement to Amy, who wasn't sure if he were good enough. He tried to escape the distortion, lying down in a guest bedroom upstairs, staring at the paisley walls, avoiding the requisite after-dinner cigar talk. Sometimes he hid in the lavatory, penis wilting, even the stream of his piss a pitiable trickle. When Muriel insisted he join the others, he came, but misbehaved. The judge chided him for propping his elbows on the table, for not spreading the napkin in his lap, for chewing with his mouth open, and for forgetting the "ladies first" rule.

"You don't open the door for your own wife," the judge snapped, "but you'll damn well open it for mine."

In the immense shadow the judge cast, Edwin was many things: beleaguered workhand, failed lawyer, farmer's son, opportunistic leach, small child most of all. And so it was little wonder that occasional nips from the liquor bottle became secretive swills. Especially when he arrived in Washington to find out that his patent had been filed by someone else, two years prior. Tail between his legs, Edwin returned home, where Amy complained about a bill for delinquent property taxes. It was the stamped with the words "Last Notice." There was no money left in the coffers. Edwin sold some of his old law books to stave off the collectors—the same books his father-in-law had purchased for him. There was a small satisfaction in that, in casting them out of the house.

Before the wrenching fall of the family's status, before the skimping, before intermittent drinking turned to habit, before the evasion and long silences and sobbing and decision to live apart, there was a moment. A.E. had committed it to memory. A debonair, criminally handsome young man stood in a dark alcove shining his shoes. He was many things. To his eldest daughter, he was only daring.

∗ ∗ ∗

A.E. received her first formal flight instructions from another girl: Neta Snook. Snook was exactly how a young woman fond of flying should look, A.E. thought. There was something brazen about the grease marks on her smooth skin. A.E. loved the way she spoke of combustion engines and farm tractors the way other girls might speak of perfume or hair ribbons. Most impressive about Neta was her easy rapport with boys, who appeared to think it perfectly natural that this messy-haired sprite should know more about flying than they did, and indeed, was right to scold them when they couldn't keep up with her during their lessons.

The trip to the airfield, where A.E. received instructions from her Snook and logged in flying time, was a long one. She would repeat it scores of times in the months ahead. She took the streetcar, sitting in the back, where she could observe the other passengers discreetly. She took the car to the end of the line. From there it was three miles to the airfield, a walk through dense neighborhoods that thinned to the odd farm-house and finally to open land. She carried with her the heavy book on aeronautics Snook had suggested. She borrowed it again and again from the library, and eventually considered it her own, even leaving pencil notes in the margins.

A.E. often took off her riding boots and socks on the walk to and fro. The tall wands of grass left fine cuts along her ankles that would itch later. She never felt them at the time. She was always exuberant on these walks. This was because she knew her destination was the sky. Never before and never again would life feel quite as purposeful. In her mouth the air tasted like honeyed milk. The sun beat ecstatically on her face. Often she would run the last half-mile, crying from a happiness that was so clean it washed straight out of her.

Her long hair would whip behind her, in the beginning. Then, week to week, it became shorter. She cut an inch here and there, so that the change was not very conspicuous. The waves crawled up her back, to her shoulders, way up about her chin, and finally, around her cheeks. Her own family hardly noticed the evolution. The tall, slim girl who was always in a rush to get somewhere, cramming crackers and apples into the pockets of her jacket, dashing out the door with nary a look back, simply looked more like the person she'd always been destined to be.

*　*　*

"Cheer up, kitty kat. You've still got eight lives left." He'd said this almost jovially. Maybe he'd meant to be amusing, but all A.E. could think was that he was wildly off-mark.

In the first place, she wasn't scared of death. She refused to be frightened of the inevitable, and had decided years ago that if she must go, she'd at least do so in style. She was fully aware of the dangers of her thrilling, untested field. And if she forgot, all she had to do was look at her flying license, stamped by the Fédération Aéronautique Internationale with the number sixteen. She being the sixteenth woman to receive one.

In the second place, Noonan didn't fathom that A.E. neither wanted nor needed validation. Maybe he told his wife to "cheer up" when she burned the meat loaf in the oven. A.E., however, didn't brighten after a patronizing pat on the back. She was a world-class pilot, and she'd arrived after long years of being underestimated. She'd broken her first of many records in her twenties. In an open cockpit, the wind beating wickedly, she'd climbed to a record height despite pea-soup fog, low oxygen, and a flimsy airship. Recognizing that certain people wouldn't believe she'd made it, she'd insisted on having a barograph installed in her plane beforehand. The barograph, with its pen nib automatically rubbing on a long sheet of revolving paper, confirmed the wild fluctuations in elevation she'd experienced. Realistically, there must be a record.

And finally, Noonan hadn't the faintest idea that most of her lives were already used up. A.E. had touched down her first plane, The Canary, in all kinds of calamitous places. Neta Snook had watched her narrowly avoid weathervanes, church steeples, smokestacks, scarecrows, and antennae. She'd berated A.E. after her pupil barely survived a miserably executed landing on a cabbage patch. The Canary itself was hardly air-worthy. Neta said it belonged in a junkyard and warned A.E. not to buy it. It had nothing going for it: short wingspan, poor horsepower, a convulsive engine. A.E. was nevertheless charmed by its exuberantly cheerful color. She had to have it. During her time with The Canary, she'd managed to use up all its luck, and sell it in the nick of time. The plane's next owner got himself killed on his virgin flight.

Others would pass, too, where she'd tread. There was her friend, Peter Barnes, who had urged her to invest in a gypsum mine he'd acquired. During a visit to the mine, a violent rainstorm cut short her tour. She left in one truck, Peter in another. She made it over a bridge and into safety, but the same bridge did not hold up for Peter. Floodwaters tore it down, sending him into the churning river below. In Oakland, A.E. had her picture taken with a flight lieutenant by the name of Ulm. He disappeared a few days later en route from Honolulu to Australia, and despite an extensive search, his body was never recovered. And then there was Will Rogers, a pilot she admired. Days after he said kind things about her in a newspaper column, his plane stalled abruptly, 300 feet over the Alaskan wilderness.

In response to these disasters, Amelia wrote and rewrote her will. She penned farewell letters. She kept meticulous records of her debts and assets. She stacked her individual records on top of one another, hoping to build a legacy. She tracked her menstruation with the same strident attention she paid to storm patterns. In her life, as on her plane, she avoided excess weight. She sighed deeply on her birthdays and accepted fancy invitations. Looking in the mirror, she touched the hollows beneath her eyes, but didn't bother searching for other signs of impending old age. She knew.

Really, Noonan had nerve to think she had any leeway left at all.

* * *

In her prior life, before she'd become The Aviatrix, A.E. had worked at a telephone company and been a nurse's aid. Briefly, she'd decided she ought to be a doctor and done a stint in medical school. She'd hauled gravel in a big truck. She'd shuffled around New York in trousers. She'd thought about becoming a novelist, for about five days. She'd gone to school for commercial photography, but given up the venture when the money didn't come in. She'd used her random gift for contortion and tried out for a circus: The Bringlebright Traveling Show, featuring The Astounding Lor Cole, Finest Wirewalker on Earth. The ringmaster had said he'd hire her if she were willing to wear a skimpy swimming suit and a rhinestone tiara. She'd declined.

"Very well then," he'd replied, not quite contritely. "Forget the tiara."

"Still, with regret, no."

After so many false starts, she was ready. Even before G.P.

asked the question, in her mind, she'd said "yes." Yes to an adventure that could end in only two ways. Yes to an endeavor that had already killed a number of hardened pilots. She told hardly anyone, not even her mother, but she never doubted for a second that she would go.

The rules were as followed, G.P. explained.

She would be billed thusly: Amelia Earhart: the first woman to cross the Atlantic.

She must keep her reputation clean. No scandals, no affairs.

She mustn't leak news of the flight. Copycats were getting smarter, and faster, all the time.

She must study Charles Lindberg and do her best to exude a similar air.

She must sign a contract holding no one liable but herself.

She must remain poised with the press.

She must learn to pose properly for photographs.

Finally, she would not be allowed to fly.

In her seat, A.E. held herself very still. "So I'm to be merely a passenger?"

"Yes, that's right."

"Why me?" she asked. To her own ears, her voice sounded even and mild. "If you don't need a pilot, you could choose any girl. Or maybe you'd rather a mannequin?"

He chuckled humorlessly and cleared his throat. "Miss Earhart, you'll be crossing an entire ocean in a cramped vessel which will be tossed about like a paper airplane. You won't exactly be sitting around with a parasol, touching up your lipstick. You'll be jumpy, sleep-deprived, and anxious, like the rest of the crew. And like the rest of the crew, you'll be expected to pull your weight and keep your wits about you. Your skills and experience will be welcome onboard, even if they won't be utilized—directly." He managed to sound firm, yet also vaguely complimentary.

"But I can fly. I want to fly. I *ought* to fly."

"And you will," he said, his eyes awash with excitement. "After you've gotten your name out there, you can do whatever you please. You can even let me help you, if you'd like."

A.E. was aware that she was dealing with a huckster in the order of the ringmaster. But at least she was under no illusion. She was also under no pretense that she was replaceable. Surely there were other female pilots who fit the bill: young, attractive, competent, and sufficiently reminiscent of Charles Lindberg. Back very straight, chin very high, she stared appraisingly at this stranger: George Palmer Putnam. She yearned to say something sharp, something that would puncture his arrogance and keep him thinking well into the night. But she knew that when opportunity beckons, you follow. You bite your tongue, put on your hat and overcoat, and shut the door behind you.

* * *

Upon take-off of the Friendship, the vessel that would carry her across the Atlantic, A.E. understood G.P.'s point about keeping her wits about her. The latch on the cabin door came undone as the plane rolled down the runway. A.E. managed to grab the door as it swung open. She struggled to keep it closed against the wild tug and suck of wind until one of her shipmates, Slim Gordon, leapt out of the copilot's seat to help. The two tied one end of a rope around the latch, the other to a huge gasoline tin, hoping that the weight of the tin would keep the door in place. It didn't. As the plane rose, the door flung wide, dragging its anchor across the floor. A.E. pounced on the tin like a cat. She wasn't heavy enough to keep it from its wayward slide, however. The portal into wide-open air approached with sickening speed. Maybe she'd be able to brace her feet against the doorframe, maybe she wouldn't. She didn't have time to think it over.

Gordon surged forward again, face white and sweaty. He grabbed her and threw her aside. At the same time, the tin rolled, sideswiping his calves, knocking him off balance. One of his feet grazed the door ledge. A blast of air ballooned the legs of his pants. Wind slapped his face. He swayed perilously. He would have fallen out, surely, if the plane had not, by chance, tilted at that exact moment. As he fell back on his rear, gravity slammed shut the door long enough for A.E. and Gordon to tie it again, this time securely. They shared a deep breath, a quick, disbelieving smile. Gordon rubbed his calf and gave her a funny little bow. She nodded, still jarred, and sat herself down on another tin. Taking out her stenographer's notebook, she forced herself to make an entry, though her hand was shaking. She remembered G.P.'s crack about the parasol and lipstick. Boy, if he could see her now. Fishing about in the pocket of her leather coat, she located her compact and powdered her nose. She was surprised at how level her gray eyes appeared in the mirror.

*　*　*

The rest of the journey would be no easier than the first few minutes. The pilot, Bill Stultz, drank heavily at the end of every leg. The plane was too heavy, and all excess weight had to be jettisoned: a movie camera, wool blankets, the clothing that the crew didn't have on their backs. Even so, the plane could barely lift its plump pontoons during water take-offs. A.E. yearned to take the controls. Her exasperation increased when she found a bottle of scotch wedged between a tool kit and a box of spare parts. She almost stormed the cockpit. G.P.'s rules didn't keep her back: she simply knew she didn't have enough clout.

Three thousand miles later, in Wales, that changed. When the plane touched down in a small fishing village, she secured her place on the front pages of newspapers around the world. Thousands of strangers learned her name. The girl who had put every nickel into buying that rattletrap Canary was chauffeured in a Rolls Royce. As the car rolled slowly through hysterical throngs, autograph-seekers thrust pieces of paper through the open windows. The best hotels begged her to stay in their rooms, gratis. Parties pivoted around her presence. Strangers wanted to marry her. George Bernard Shaw invited her to tea. The Prince of Wales blushed when he asked her to dance.

She'd left America with a suede satchel she could fling over her shoulder. She came back with two new steamer trunks packed full of new clothes. The fashion houses loved her figure. It was perfect for draping, they raved, encouraging her to wear their latest things: tight-cinching belts, French gloves, shawls and capes and scarves in the kind of hot, loud hues she normally avoided.

Stateside, G.P. meticulously orchestrated her welcome-home party. In New York she was propped high in the back of a convertible between Gordon and a stiff, sullen Stultz. She was the headliner in a parade that rolled exuberantly from Battery to Broadway. In truth she could hardly digest the commotion and adulation. She couldn't see past the tickertape; the torn-up telephone book pages flung out of windows, drifting about her like snowflakes; the emotional, even tangible longing for a brave, wholesome heroine in an America falling on hard times. That she might be the desired protagonist filled her with dread. For god's sake, she hadn't even piloted the plane.

When the reporters swarmed her, she gave Stutz the lion's share of credit. But they didn't hear her. They were love-struck, blinded by the bright bob of her hair, her profile worthy of coinage. The flashbulbs popped. Attractive in person, she was glorious in photos: statuesque, triumphant, an entire nation's raw potential poured into female form.

The cameras followed her faithfully to Boston, where A.E. reunited with her mother and sister. Her decision not to inform them about the transatlantic trip had done injury. Muriel was, by turns, weepy and angry. Amy had aged visibly. Time and penance might redeem A.E. But she was not willing to give either. Every member of her immediate family was irreparably broken. She knew if she let them, they would break her too.

Sadly, there were more old ties to cut. Sam Chapman, her longtime chum, the man who yearned to marry her, must be sacrificed. For years he had followed her as she'd tramped from place to place. He'd loved her deeply, and loyally. She'd never doubted that. But she'd kept him in her back pocket for too long now. She was 31 years old, hardly an ingénue.

In Boston Sam called her at the hotel. Full of boyish giddiness he stopped by her room, looking the same as he always did: hopeful and desperate. She wondered if he saw the change in her. The daisies he grasped in his hands seemed rustic and touching amid a sea of expensive bouquets.

"I'm sorry, Sam, truly. I wish you wouldn't look so eager."

He argued, like he had in the past, but she was decisive. This time she didn't leave room for negotiation. Less than an hour later he left, the daisies wilting in his hands. The corners of her mouth were raw from an awkward, too-rough kiss. Sam's sudden, uncustomary burst of passion hadn't fooled either of them.

Late into the night A.E. tossed in the cold hotel bed. She cried, but more out of exhaustion than sorrow. At 3 a.m., eyes wide open, she called G.P.

"Who is this?" he asked groggily.

"I know I ought to be grateful," she began without introduction. "Only, well, I feel so sulky. I'm a pilot, not this idol they've made me out to be. It's one heck of a predicament. Don't get me wrong—the chocolate-covered cherries, the telegram from the President—they're swell. They're dandy.

But, well . . . I'd rather be flying."

In a quiet tone, so as not to wake his wife, G.P. soothed her. He said all the things she wanted to hear. The next day, she woke up chilled, but fresh. She had no more doubts. Today she would return to New York City, to Madison Square Garden. She would continue on her five-city publicity blitz by giving a nationwide broadcast on NBC. If there were any Americans who hadn't heard of her, they would soon. By tomorrow night the sponsors would be lined up at her door, G.P. had promised.

Then she could fly to her heart's content.

* * *

G.P. had made the invitation: Come live with me and my wife in Rye. Write a book about your transatlantic voyage there, in peace, uninterrupted. I'll publish it when you're done.

She asked if G.P.'s wife, Dorothy, were accepting of this idea.

She loves company, he assured her.

Accused of wanderlust by her sister, A.E. had done more than her fair share of traveling. She didn't mind sleeping on a sofa or a cot and eating foods she couldn't name. She was an undemanding guest. As long as the Putnams wanted to host her, she didn't see the harm in accepting G.P.'s offer.

He picked her up himself from Grand Central Terminal. They talked the entire ride. In terms of the book, G.P. wanted her to concentrate on the two detailed notebooks she had filled on the voyage; names, dates, and flight specifics he had amassed; a couple of transcribed interviews with Stultz. She was inclined to agree with G.P.'s logic: it was faster to recycle than to start from scratch. G.P. was candid about his expectations. If they pulled the book off in time, sales would meet or exceed the Lindbergh volume, his publishing house's previous coup.

"The motto from now on is 'two weeks or bust,'" he told her.

"Two weeks?"

"It's been done before." He was staring dead ahead at flying highway.

"Even for you, that's cockamamie. No one can write a book in two weeks."

"Well, you'll have a head start. I had an employee create an editorial skeleton. Only a few thousand words, nothing grand. But it does include all the features you need to flesh out: reactions to the force of the Atlantic, thoughts on commercial aviation, why you skirts are so up in arms about equal rights."

"You had an employee write about my experiences, from my perspective?"

"That's right."

He took his eyes off the road long enough to glance at her. He was pleased to see an amused smile.

"How enterprising of you."

Amelia dangled her arm out the window of the speeding car. Her fingers skittered on the current. In this way she and G.P. pulled into the drive of the Putnams' Spanish Mission-style home in Rye. It was exactly how he'd described it: remotely situated, serene, and sprawling: sixteen rooms and six baths.

The perfect place to be productive, she decided, satisfied that she'd come.

She'd been mildly worried about meeting Dorothy, but took to her at once. There wasn't a hint of reserve or inscrutability about G.P.'s wife. She shook A.E.'s hand vigorously, then pulled her by the wrist to show off the house: every room, every crevice, even the cluttered closets. A.E. liked her effusiveness.

"Nothing is off-limits," Dorothy told the aviatrix. "The cupboard at midnight, the backgammon table, it's all yours. Whatever you like."

Amelia got a kick out of her bedroom, which had been decorated with an outdoor enthusiast's aesthetic. A massively antlered moose's head hung on one wall, watercolors of fowl and trout on another. The colors of the walls and trim and bedding suited A.E.: hunter green and washed blue. She would have liked to spend more time here, but G.P. insisted she hole up in the library. There, Dorothy, her dark hair always coiffed, administered a constant flow of cocoa and cookies.

Contented, the aviatrix dug in, working 14-hour days. The ghostwriter, god bless his intrepid heart, had dared to describe the colors of the sky A.E. had seen over the Atlantic. He waxed poetic on her feelings as the Friendship touched down in Wales. All the phoniness made her queasy. She went about correcting false notes, filling in the holes, and wondering what would have become of all this tripe had the plane not landed safely.

When he wasn't at the New York office, G.P. was standing in back of her chair in the library. His demands for progress reports were incessant. The "two weeks or bust" rule wasn't applesauce, apparently. For fun, she kept a tally of his odes to timeliness: "You have to act while the story is hot, not while it's cooling on the counter." "Every day that passes is a nail in the coffin of the public's interest." "Time is money, and we're already a quarter past." "Shake a leg, lass, shake a leg."

When she got to bed each night, the sentences she'd written during the day floated in her brain. She couldn't will them away. Sometimes she awakened with new paragraphs, whole and clean, better than any she'd constructed by day. Groggily, she wrote them down on a notepad she kept on the bedside table. The lamplight, a wan orb in the black country night, made her eyes ache. She'd need reading glasses if she kept up.

The air felt very still in Rye. Not just quiet, but heavy and hebetudinous. She missed the sound of automobiles and street talk and children screeching and just, well, action. The scratch of her pencil and G.P.'s jabbering were just about the only noises she heard, and so the rap on her door, late one night, made her jump. It was G.P., stripped of his get-up-and-go oomph and pinstripe suit, dressed instead in skittishness and flannel pajamas. He made no apology for appearing in her doorway at an obscene hour, and had no excuse. And yet she wasn't in the least surprised to see him.

Some men buy the women they are fond of jewelry. Some buy furs. George Palmer Putnam had bought her a plane. It was the same one an acquaintance, the aviatrix Lady Mary Heath, had famously flown from Cape Town to London. Heath had put it up for auction, and G.P. had made the winning bid. A.E. couldn't believe his generosity. He explained that it was customary in publishing to bequeath a present on a new client. Consider it an advance on the soon-to-be-finished book.

"Hi, George. Come to offer me cookies and a glass of warm milk?"

"It's too late for that junk," he harrumphed, scratching at his elbow. Seconds flickered by.

"You can come in," she offered.

She couldn't see him very well, but as he edged closer, tentatively, she could smell him: tobacco and talcum, with a beery undercurrent. The lamplight strained to reach him, and he, like a criminal wary of searchlights, evaded it. He got as far as the bed, touching the quilt, which sported quails and rabbits, with his fingertips.

"I heard a noise," he mumbled. "I had to make sure everything was—safe."

"And is it?" She rubbed her eyes and put the notebook on her lap aside.

"I hope so."

"Don't you worry. No marauders here—except the moose."

He opened his mouth. Nothing came out—a most unusual turn of events. Still, he made no motion to leave.

"Are you sure you're all right, George?"

Still he didn't move. Still his mouth was immobile and agape, which made him look a little dopey. Rarely was George Palmer Putnam speechless, but that was exactly what he appeared to be.

"Good night, Amelia," he said finally.

"Sleep tight."

He shut the door and didn't open it again for the rest of her stay.

* * *

A week into writing *20 Hrs. 30 Min.: Our Flight in the Friendship*, as G.P. had anointed the book, Amelia felt more confident. She was confident enough to take frequent breaks. These were spent with one of the Putnams' sons, David, who was home from boarding school, and with other guests who drifted in and out of the house. Mainly, though, A.E. spent time with her hostess. G.P. had been right: Dorothy was most comfortable with company. She preferred the eccentric, famous, and rich, not necessarily in that order.

If A.E. found companionship in Dorothy, Dorothy found a fledgling. George's skinny, quiet protégé was a nice girl, if unexceptional (Dorothy couldn't understand all the fuss). At least A.E. was easygoing. She readily joined Dorothy during her late day strolls in the garden. As they walked, A.E. asked about the shallow bowls set near some vegetable plants. A dozen were half-buried in the earth, their rims level with the ground. They were filled with dirty brown water. A.E. thought their presence unsightly—strange since the garden was otherwise well-kept.

Were they miniature birdbaths, Amelia asked politely.

"God, no. They're full of beer. Good German lager!"

A.E. stopped in her tracks, laughing. "Are you trying to get the birds drunk?"

"No, the slugs."

"Inebriated slugs!"

"Just dead ones," Dorothy said. "They slide into the bowls and drown, and my poor, tattered cabbages stand a chance."

"It's not a bad way to go, I suppose."

"I've tried everything else. I've paid the boys to pick them off and throw them into the pond. They must have gills because they find their way back. I've poured salt on them, but that's a bit cruel. I've squished them, and cut them on broken eggshells. We're in an all-out war, the slugs and I, and I'm afraid I'm losing."

"Well, nobody can accuse you of a lack of commitment."

"Oh no, not when it comes to my cabbages. Anyone who pillages them deserves what's coming."

Amelia wondered whether she'd been underestimating Dorothy, who seemed, now, mightier than before.

"Can I ask you something?" the aviatrix asked hesitantly.

"Of course—anything."

A.E.'s sunburned face went a deeper shade of brown. "Did you always think that you'd have what you have now: your marriage, your boys, your garden? This kind of life? Oh my, I hope I don't sound intrusive or strange. I question myself every so often, my future, that is, and like to know how other women have planned things."

Dorothy dug the heel of her boot into the soil. They were good Italian boots, calfskin, expensive. She liked shoes, and seldom favored one pair for long, but she'd had these resoled twice. Her husband couldn't understand why she walked her garden in her best shoes, and she couldn't explain it to him.

"I knew my future was with George the minute I met him. The second minute, at any rate."

"Well, I admire the life you've made."

Dorothy smiled distractedly. She looked at A.E., but didn't seem to be actually seeing her. "I don't know if I'm deserving of admiration. There are pros and cons to every decision, and being settled can mean stagnation, if one is not careful."

She checked her heel, rubbing off a bit of muck with her glove, and walked on, Amelia scurrying to keep up with her. Dorothy Putnam knew the layout of her garden by heart and could have given a tour of it blindfolded. Here and there she snapped blooms and blades, leaves and berried sprigs. Her fingers busily knit them into a tidy, compact bouquet.

"You've probably guessed that I'm putting off domestic duty," Amelia confessed. "I'm a born procrastinator. Take the book, for example. I'm past deadline already."

This time it was Dorothy who made sure to sound polite. She picked off ferny bits of dill from the bouquet and let the breeze carry them off her fingers: "Yes, I've heard that."

"Today makes three days past the 'due date.'"

"You don't say?"

"I'm almost there, though, I can see the light at the end of the tunnel."

"Well, that's good."

Dorothy pressed the bouquet into Amelia's hands. The aviatrix took a sniff and had to stifle a sneeze. She was surprised by its rank odor. Dorothy had created an unharmonious potpourri: nose-stinging marigolds, milkweed, oniony chive straws, globe thistle, and sweet-looking lilies that happened to stink like manure.

"Pretty, isn't it? I want you to have it," Dorothy said. "I've been meaning to infuse your room with a little femininity."

* * *

In the end it took A.E. three weeks, exactly. That was good enough for George. He always figured in a cushion. Writers and women were notoriously unreliable, especially in combination.

He read the draft in seclusion while A.E. paced nervously in the library, impressed that by sheer habit of staring she'd managed to memorize the order of books on three shelves. When G.P. arrived finally, manuscript in hand, he had a satisfied smile. A.E. laughed brightly, skipping about like a child let outdoors after a long rain.

"Edits will be minimal," he told her. "We'll be able to proof and copyedit this by Wednesday, and send it to print as a priority."

To celebrate, he took Amelia, Dorothy, and David out to dinner. The passengers took several minutes to decide who ought to sit where in the car. Dorothy tsked her berry-colored lips and insisted that her husband let a woman drive for once. A.E. agreed cheerfully, volunteering for the task, then appointing Dorothy to ride upfront as her "official Rye navigator." David chimed in. As the youngest, he had rights too, inalienable rights, and driving was one of them.

George, who'd been dreaming of a good rib eye since noon and skipped lunch in anticipation of one, grew irritated by all the hullabaloo. Determined not to waste more time, he climbed behind the wheel. The chatter and good-natured accusations turned to jeers, but by then he had started the engine, which rumbled at the same volume as his tummy. He yelled like he meant it: "Any more of this racket and you three are footing the bill!" Even Dorothy wasn't sure if he meant it. When George was hungry, or cross, there was no telling. And so the protesters clammed up, and clambered into the seats that were closest to them.

Dinner was uneventful. It was on the way back, when they were too full to be lively, that things went wrong. G.P. was speeding along a winding, wooded road. The women were slumped in gorged comfort in the back. David accompanied his father upfront, glad to be close to the steering wheel. George was taking a detour. He didn't like to backtrack if he could help it. He'd driven this way another time, years ago, and vaguely remembered its landmarks. The wine he'd downed at dinner stilted his reaction time, but he was concentrating hard. When the animal appeared, bold and bristly-black, he was annoyed. It shouldn't have been there, not on such a dark night on such a dark road. It had no business crossing here, exactly where his car was going. He was annoyed, too, that he didn't know what this creature was—real or a shadowy illusion—only that it was in his way.

He braked hard. The tires screeched as they tried to cling to the road. An audible gulp squeaked up from David. First came the shrill scream of rubber losing traction, then the pulpy thud of collision. David breathed a word: "deer." But Amelia knew it wasn't. It was something smaller, an opossum or raccoon, something too diminutive to brace itself against the car's heft, something that with better luck could have slipped under the vehicle altogether.

She was the first one out of the car. The others were still stunned and achy-slow. Dorothy had her hands in David's hair, her voice repeating, "Are you all right? Are you all right?"

Amelia felt the kick of wind in her face, but this was nothing compared to what she felt in open-cockpit planes. She followed the path of the headlights, relieved at first when she saw fur—for couldn't it have been a child?—then a nauseating guilt. The beams caught a metallic flicker: the shine of a collar. The victim, no anonymous wild animal, was instead a cat. Her nausea increased when she saw its neck, bent like a taxidermy experiment. Fur matted with sticky blood, the cat's flank heaved.

"Oh, don't touch it, dear," Dorothy said. She stood now next to A.E., who squatted. David was at her side, looking younger than his years, and holding his mother's hand. "Who knows where it's been."

"It's still alive," A.E. said flatly. "Do you have a blanket?

I need to wrap it in something."

G.P. was visible now, looming beyond the halo of the head-lights, his breath heavy. He rubbed his brow. No longer annoyed, he felt guilty and impatient. He just wanted to get home. The sooner they got there, the sooner he could forget. The more distance he could get between the car and this sad broken creature, the better for everyone.

"Amelia, leave it. It's done," he said.

"It's someone's pet. We can't leave it."

Her resoluteness stirred Dorothy. "She's right, George." She unwound the heavy brocade shawl from around her shoulders righteously. "Here, Amelia, use this."

This gesture seemed a further assault on George's conscience, and moreover his manliness, a ruse by the women in his life to totally eradicate his dignity. Rather roughly, he wrapped the shawl around his wife again, and pulled off his sports coat. He was mindful of the fact that it was expensive, and nearly new: a ridiculous sacrifice on behalf of road-kill.

"Let me do it," he said gruffly, kneeling next to Amelia.

"I will," she insisted. She spread the jacket on the ground, then lifted the cat as gently as she could. She wondered, shame-fully, if its insides would spill out. In her hands the animal felt jelly-fish wobbly. Its head listed. Its back legs were dead weight. She swaddled it and gingerly searched its collar for tags.

"What a shame," Dorothy said, her voice higher than normal, and sentimental. "Someone loved it."

"*Loves* it," David corrected.

"There's nothing to identify it," Amelia said.

"George, who lives around here?" Dorothy asked.

"How the hell should I know?" He was not pleased by this turn of events. He was cold without his jacket, and could see that he'd need to hustle this crew along if they were ever going to get home. Without a leader, they'd be standing here all night, holding a feline vigil.

"Well, I don't know why you're up-in-arms," replied Dorothy. "You're not the one we should feel sorry for."

"Pity my front tires—they took a hit."

"Dad!" David cried.

"Oh, George, really, that was in very poor taste."

"I didn't see the darn thing. It came out of nowhere. Who could have seen it?"

"I saw it," David said dolefully.

"You saw a *deer*."

"I think it's best if we just stay quiet and calm," Amelia said. When she carried the cat back to the car, the others followed, to G.P.'s relief. "Let's just get back safely so we can ring a veterinarian. Do you know of one, Dorothy?"

"We used to have one for Fergus," David said flatly.

"Fergus was our dog," Dorothy explained. "He passed away last year. Dr. Fricke was our vet. He doesn't live far from us, over on Neela Street. I still have his number in my book."

"Do you think he'll respond at this hour?" A.E. asked.

"Oh, yes, he's very caring."

Back behind the wheel, G.P. leaned his head side to side, trying to work out the kink in his neck. He felt a headache coming on. He'd felt it earlier, too, when his rib eye had arrived too rare. He'd had to send it back twice. In the end, he'd eaten it overcooked.

He drove at half his normal speed, wishing his son would quit sniffling. It wasn't like David was crying, his boys were tough that way, but still the noise was incessant and aggravating. In the backseat, the cat felt heavy in A.E.'s lap. Its odor filled the car: sharp, gassy, intestinal. She was used to bad smells: gas fumes in the cockpit, sweat, the green funk of fear, bodily accidents that couldn't wait till landing. She had a tolerance.

In retrospect, A.E. thought she could have identified the exact moment the cat died. It didn't let out a sound, or move.

It simply felt lighter in her lap, and colder, very suddenly, like its life was storming out abruptly. She stopped stroking its head.

George pulled into the driveway, and parked the car in the garage. They got out and huddled in a tense circle. Amelia had rewrapped the cat into a stealth parcel, its head hidden for David's sake. He announced that the cat could sleep in his room. Dorothy had a sense of things. She was watching the way A.E. held the cat mummy-tight, how her eyes seemed more weary than concerned now.

She said, "Why don't you get ready for bed, Davy-boy, and we'll take care of the cat."

"You're going to call Dr. Glasz, aren't you?"

"Off to bed you go. We'll call him."

David agreed with reluctance, and tramped off. Meanwhile, the adults lingered in the garage, George rubbing his hands and brooding, Dorothy glancing at Amelia before saying, "There are a couple of shovels in the corner. George, why don't you take care of that part? I'll phone Dr. Fricke anyway, in case he knows who the owner was. Such a shame." She unclipped her earrings and slipped them into her pocket. With the exception of her naked earlobes, she looked as fresh and polished as she had before dinner.

"Maybe we should wait until morning to bury it," Amelia said. "Let David think it put up a valiant fight."

"Good idea, Amelia. It would be okay to leave it here for the night, don't you think? No sense taking it inside now."

The women found a box and deposited the cat's stiffening body, then bid each other goodnight with brisk kisses to the cheeks. They departed without saying anything more to George, because they were tired, or to punish him, or both. When it was quiet, he stared for a time at the box. It had pictures of bell peppers on the sides and the words Fresh! Wholesome! Tasty! Poor taste, indeed, he thought. He left and walked to a guest bedroom on the opposite end of the house. He had wanted to create distance, real geographic space, between himself and the accident, but it had followed him home. Now all he could do was venture into the room farthest from the garage, where there was no fireplace, where his papers were not scattered, where there was neither telephone nor cigar nor pen. No creature comforts. G.P. was not a man prone to self-punishment. He didn't subscribe to contrition inspired by religion, human error, or the confounding expectations of the fairer sex. But he did feel sorry, quite sorry, about what had happened, and this chilly, far-flung room felt like the right place to be. There was a slim tract between the bed and bureau and he paced it, wondering how he could make it up to whoever had owned that darned cat. Maybe he'd buy them another one. Maybe buy two and give one to David.

★　★　★

When A.E. awoke the next morning, she wondered if the dead cat actually existed or if it were a dream. She decided it was probably real, and grew certain of it when she came down for breakfast to find Dorothy at the kitchen table in complete mourning attire: black dress, black stockings, and pointy black slingbacks. Perched in front of her on the table was a black hat: a gauzy crinoline confection with a cobwebby veil. David was eating a poached egg with his fingers. He was cheerful, with no trace of last night's misery. He announced, rather buoyantly, that the cat had died during the night and now they were going to bury it. He'd been given the assignment of making a tomb-stone. Egg in one hand, he gesticulated to Amelia how he planned to carve an inscription with a chisel and a hammer on a flat, rectangular stone he'd found down by the pond. It was a perfect tombstone-type stone, as David explained it, big and rectangular and a solemn shade of gray.

"What time is the service?" Amelia asked.

"Ten o'clock," Dorothy said. She daintily dug a spoon into the top of an egg on a little silver stand. She nodded to Amelia to join them at the table. "David is preparing the grave marker, as you know, and I'm arranging the flowers. Amelia, would you do us the honor of reading a piece of poetry?"

"That would be my pleasure," she replied, pulling out a chair and stacking triangles of toast onto her plate. "My own poem? Or can I choose one from someone with a little more talent?"

"Whichever you wish."

"What about the gravesite? Has that been decided?"

"We've picked a spot in the garden, beside one of the old apple trees. A nice spot: shady and leafy and peaceful. George is digging the hole now."

David looked up from a clutter of eggshells and blinked. Amelia poured herself a cup of tea. "Well, it sounds as if everything is in order."

With the book behind her, she felt free to be leisurely and languid, at least for a few hours. She'd be leaving Rye that afternoon, headlong into a new slew of tasks G.P. had prepared for her. Through with her packing, she thought she would like to direct her energy into the search for a poem. After breakfast she searched the library's collection. She spent more time than was called for, and decided, at last, on a poem by Edna St. Vincent Millay. It was equal parts love letter, fond farewell, and hard-nosed brush with reality. After reading the poem twice aloud, she grew unexpectedly teary.

At ten on the nose, David transported the bell pepper box to the deep square hole George had dug. Amelia approved of the location and of the stocky, sturdy, knobby apple tree at the garden's edge. Yonder, the garden tapered into a bushy thicket, and beyond that, woodland. Next spring, David said, he'd plant some roses over the grave, or some catnip. A splendid idea, his mother told him.

Amelia read the poem she had rehearsed. Afterward, she took a moment to digest a cross Dorothy had woven out of weeping willow whips. It hung over the grave from the apple tree. She looked at David's grave marker. Its underside was still wet and green-mossy from its life near the pond. It had two large, clumsy letters only: an R. and I., but Dorothy and A.E. praised David's work lavishly. A.E. noted the bouquets in good glass vases on either side of the hole, and how Dorothy's veil fluttered about her eyes, making her look like the femme fatal from a dime novel.

"Thank you, Amelia," Dorothy said, after a lull, and lifted a handkerchief to her lips. A.E. was surprised that her new friend was crying—that she had given in to the melancholy that was real, but also very much their creation—and was then relieved to realize that Dorothy was not sniffling but stifling a laugh. David, bewildered, glowered at his mother, which made her giggle outright. The corners of Amelia's mouth rose, in spite of her attempt to stop them, and now David's eyes took on a wild, accusatory shape.

"Sorry, Davy," Dorothy said. "It's just. . .I was overcome."

George had opted not to participate in the ceremony. He observed it instead from a window in his study. From here he could see that his wife looked dramatic and glamorous, Amelia like a sharecropper in her coveralls, and his son taller by the second. The three had lined up in front of the hole. He'd had difficulty digging it. The ground near the apple tree was rocky, craggy, resistant to intrusion. He'd needed a pick and hoe in addition to a shovel. He'd done a decent job, though, had a couple of plum calluses to prove it, and felt sufficiently absolved of last night's guilt as he watched the three mourners. Dorothy made the sign of the cross, after which David pitched shovelfuls of dirt into the grave, packing the earth into some semblance of what it had been.

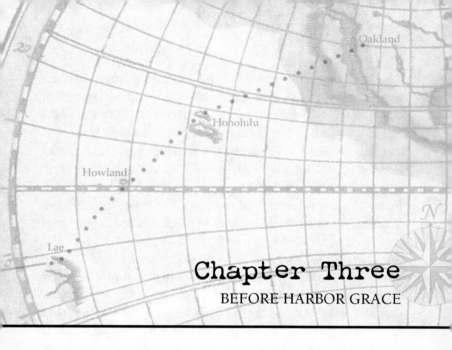

Chapter Three
BEFORE HARBOR GRACE

A.E. CONSIDERED ALBERT, THE MAN HER SISTER HAD married, to be a taker. A hanger-on. To be perfectly blunt, a good-for-nothing. Upon their nuptials, A.E. had clung to a grim but persistent hope that, at last, another member of the clan would contribute financially. This hope dimmed considerably once Muriel and Albert asked her for a $2500 loan on their mortgage.

A.E. had sent it dutifully, asking for a receipt in the form of legal documentation. A record would increase the likelihood of repayment. To date, no paperwork had arrived, only a thank you note with too many exclamation points. A.E. saw the balance of her bank account dwindle. There was still a comfortable sum, to be sure, but she liked to feel secure. G.P. had more engagements for her, nothing she really wanted to take on, nor had time to. Now she would agree to all of them.

With her weathered complexion and uncanny composure, A.E. was frequently misinterpreted as robust. Her voice rang steady over the radio waves. Photographs caught neither fray nor fever. A ready smile went a long way. In actuality, she was only moderately strong, with no more reserves than most. She had a handful of tricks to rejuvenate: her thermos of cocoa, a sip of tomato soup, firm slaps to her cheeks. She bore the weight, mostly, through a steadfast refusal to quit anything she'd started.

After the spree of commitments following the loan to Muriel, A.E.'s exhaustion manifested itself in odd places. Her tongue ached when she drank cold water. It seethed under salty foods. Examining it in a mirror, she was dismayed to see bald, inflamed patches, randomly scoured of texture. Over the following days, these patches changed position, healing in one place, then sprouting up in another.

"Benign Migratory Glossitis," Doctor Brannigan told her. "My first instinct was to think the condition has to do with your travel. A foreign disease. However, looking more carefully, I think the diagnosis is less exotic. The common term for what you have is Geographic Tongue. It's nothing serious. Certainly not a cancer. It's recognized as a physical manifestation of fatigue and a compromised immune system. There is no cure, but the symptoms seem to abate with rest, with less stress and anxiety."

"So anyone can get it?"

Doctor Brannigan considered this. "No, I wouldn't say that. It's symptomatic of only a small percentage of the general population: two, maybe three percent. Benign Migratory Glossitis is a random illness—it's origins are not very well understood. Certain people simply seem more prone to it than others."

"Geographic Tongue," A.E. repeated.

"Fitting, given your profession."

"Very," she answered wryly.

The condition seemed to be aggravated by increased contact with her sister. A new patch appeared when Muriel complained of Amy's living at her house. No husband likes a mother-in-law sleeping in the next room, she declared. Kills the romance.

The lesion took a northerly turn when Amy asked A.E. for a monthly "support stipend." It further grew after Muriel began penning a weekly column for her local newspaper. She was paid to report on about how A.E. liked her eggs, whether she'd always had such a nose for fashion, if she liked to crochet. The columns had such titles as "Amelia Earhart: Woman Behind the Myth" and "America's Aviatrix: Earth, Sky, and Homefront." Amy assured her that Muriel's intentions were innocent. Even so, A.E.'s blood boiled.

The aviatrix was worried, too, that Muriel was pregnant again. Brazenly, A.E. sent her sister *The Doctor's Modern Manual of Marriage*: a book about birth control. To soften the gesture, she included toys, linens, and a gorgeous, never-worn camel hair coat. Still, she wasn't sorry about the book.

Whole paragraphs from *The Doctor's Modern Manual of Marriage* resurfaced in A.E.'s brain on a subsequent visit to Dr. Brannigan. This time she saw him not within the white walls of a hospital, but on the second floor of a closed-down rifle manufacturing plant. It was his second office: an off-the-record establishment. Only women entered, and they were quiet and skittish.

The aviatrix was dressed in one of her trademark outfits: cropped khaki blazer, trim trousers, riding boots, a high-collared blouse, flying wings on the lapel. Though covered head to toe, she felt a little naked as she took in the room: a couple of knocked-about chairs, a cabinet with a cluttered counter, an operating table. With its metal stirrups and leather straps, the latter reminded A.E. of a medieval torture device. She wasn't pleased to note that the stirrups were scuffed, the straps visibly stretched.

To occupy herself, she got up and looked out the window. It was mid-afternoon on a winter's day. The sun hadn't made any victory today, and was already sinking. Too early, it seemed to A.E. Though the surrounding buildings were sparsely populated, she drew the shades. She dallied at the counter, fingering the scalpel, forceps, and scissors, taking time to study the jars packed with cotton balls, gauze, bandages, and dressings. She smelled formaldehyde and rubbing alcohol, the same medley she'd gotten used to when she'd worked as a nurse's aid.

A.E. knew precisely how she'd come to be here, a three-hour's drive from Rye, in a neighborhood she would ordinarily take care to bypass, foot on the gas, in a room that was low-lit and, frankly, depressing. Month to month, she could count her intimate encounters with G.P. on one hand, sometimes on no hand at all. She must have gotten in trouble after the John Barrymore's Christmas party. She and G.P. had drunk too much champagne, were in a celebratory mood. They'd been affectionate all through the party and upon returning home G.P. had even sung her a warbling serenade. Afterward, they'd fallen asleep in a heap of blankets and pillows. A.E. hadn't taken a hot bath, rinsed herself with vinegar, or done any of the other things the manual recommended.

When Doctor Brannigan arrived, he found her still loitering about the counter, wearing her concern plainly. His expression caused her to retreat to a chair. Dispensing with pleasantries, he began rubbing the steel instruments with a handkerchief. He preempted his question, explaining he didn't mean to pry. Nevertheless, he had to ask, had she informed Mr. Putnam?

A.E. was as annoyed as she was antsy. She had hoped Doctor Brannigan would be respectful and discreet. He even looked discreet, with an any man's face. Another member of the Ninety-Nines had employed him for this procedure, and confided to A.E. that he had never uttered a word of it afterward. But now A.E. wasn't sure who Brannigan was, precisely. Why would a respectable physician moonlight in such a place?

Was he a champion of women, or a misogynist? Was he goading her? And if so, was it because she and George were prominent people and he was envious? A.E. knew for certain only that he needed cash upfront, two hundred dollars, and another twenty-five for the nurse who would be assisting. He wouldn't write down the address of this building, but mumbled it tersely. At the time, since she and Brannigan had discussed the matter during his regular hours at the hospital, A.E. had interpreted his reserve as carefulness. Now she was more skeptical.

Criminy, a rifle factory, of all places.

She deliberated. She could walk out the door right now, of course, but she was desperate to get on with things. Her condition had put her in a shabby way. She'd wrestled with the decision at the expense of meals and rest. She'd developed odd, nervous habits: counting the number of times she blinked, relentlessly shuffling her feet. The more she deliberated, the more roundabout her logic became. Yet her conclusions were consistent. She didn't like anything, or anyone, all of the time. She desired to take care of no additional family members. She didn't want to get married. And no, she hadn't told G.P., but she didn't see how this was any of Brannigan's business.

"Rest assured, doctor. This is the correct choice for both of us."

"I ask this of all my patients: take a few minutes now to assess your decision before we begin. Once the nurse arrives, and the anesthesia administered, we'll proceed quickly. I don't want you to regret anything."

"That's why I'm here, so I won't regret anything."

A.E. watched Brannigan swallow this with a flinch. She wondered when, exactly, the nurse was coming.

"I'm aware of your name recognition, Miss Earhart. And I'm aware of the perils of your profession. Air travel is a particularly dangerous field. I'm not speaking out of conjecture either. My brother was in the service—aerial combat. The stories he told me made me think the human race oughtn't leave the ground at all. And if it must, perhaps only the men should go. Let them pursue the fame, the frivolous glory. And let them shoulder the danger."

She'd heard this argument before. She had rebutted it countless times, in countless ways.

"Doctor, with all due respect, I don't see how this is relevant."

He went on boldly.

"I think I understand your psychology. Something about this aviation field gives you a thrill. More than the typical motherly and wifely pursuits. Maybe it satisfies a certain appetite other females suppress? You're a modern woman. Modern women don't follow convention—fine. But why not find another diversion, Miss Earhart? There must be another way to pacify yourself. One that will enable you to honor more traditional roles. It seems to me, from a clinical perspective, you have no good reason to fly. You're not wanting for anything, are you? A man like Mr. Putnam must be a good provider. Very good, in fact. So you fly to break records, to get your name on plaques. It's my observation that you fly to satisfy your own ego. Is that a reasonable conclusion?"

"If reasonable means misguided, then 'yes,'" she answered. She was furious, shocked, bemused, on the verge of tears, and determined not to let any of it show.

"I suppose you're one of those females who think that women should be drafted too?"

"With equality ought to come shared responsibilities, good and bad. I've always believed that, yes."

"In theory, Miss Earhart, but thank heavens this is a country that doesn't take its women for granted. We honor our women. We go to war for you. We give our lives for you. That is the American way."

"The Nineteenth Amendment to the Constitution guarantees women the right to vote. With this right come other vital responsibilities of citizenship. To defend this nation, to contribute to its betterment and sanctity, these are the responsibilities of which I speak. If the draft is included, so be it. Like men, women ought not be disqualified from aggressive military action when such action is necessary."

This declaration passed through her lips automatically. She was surprised to find herself still in the room.

"Oh come now, I would have thought you'd be more patriotic."

"I am patriotic. I'm thrilled we live in a country that grants the right to earn a living, in any profession, to all persons. I'm thrilled that America is open to change and advancement and new opportunity."

The doctor was beginning to bristle. She showed none of her own indignation, but should he have looked, Brannigan would have seen goosebumps along her upper arms. The ridge of her back tingled. She yearned to leave, but this would mean postponement, possibly cancellation. Most of all she wanted to be done with the procedure, right now. She wished it were already over, in fact, and that she was looking back at this scenario from a safe distance. Her fingers knitted themselves in her lap. Her underarms were soaking wet. She paused, thinking she'd best give Brannigan an inch, even if he didn't deserve it.

"Doctor, I appreciate your opinion. You've articulated your point—vividly. You must think you are doing right by advising me. But I've never *wanted* to have children. George has known this all along; it's not a secret. When we met, flying was my life. It still is. Perhaps, that kind of singularity makes me an aberration among females—clinically speaking."

It was ridiculous, really, that she was comforting him. Her motivation was not unselfish. If Brannigan were truly going to help her, he needed to be calm and confident. She would have to make him calm and confident.

She wondered if he gave the same spiel to other women. Perhaps she was becoming bitter, or just more shrewd, but she could see how he might have singled her out. There was prestige in being the man who delivered Amelia Earhart's baby. Certainly there was none in what they were doing.

A softening of the doctor's expression made her see he was caving in. He stopped polishing the instruments, finally. As if on cue, feet tapped lightly in the hall beyond the door. The nurse? The aviatrix was granted her wish. When the woman in white entered, the very air in the room seemed to brighten. Sweet-faced and young, she was an immediate and sympathetic counterweight to Brannigan.

Soon after, A.E. was instructed to inhale chloroform. She was also told to drink a small glass of clear, vinegary fluid. She refused a second glass, but sheepishly swallowed it after a strict look from the nurse.

"Nurse Alice," she told A.E., smiling.

A.E. thought about the name, thought about *Alice in Wonderland*, as she drifted to sleep. She would not be aware of the rambling, childish chatter she was about to engage in, nor would she remember it afterward. Doctor Brannigan dismissed her jabber, deeming it inconsequential. Under anesthesia, his patients often wept, protested, laughed, and cursed. It was to be expected at this stage, and besides, with the nurse here and his instruments ready, he was prepared to move forward. There were precise steps to follow. A regimen. Regardless of how many extractions he had performed, he must dedicate his full attention.

"It's a girl, isn't it?" A.E. asked blithely. "Can I hold her? When will you let me hold her?"

Nurse Alice, too, had heard all kinds of non sequiturs, last wishes, and secret sentiments. She could not deflect any of them as readily as the doctor, however. She touched her white cap pensively, wishing the bobby pins weren't so tight on her blonde head. She bent close to Miss Earhart, thinking that her hair smelled like wet leaves on a windy autumn day. The aviatrix's face was much more feminine than in the papers, where she seemed to Alice a bit mannish. The nurse dared to touch her cheek.

"When will we be having dinner?" A.E. asked. "I'll invite my aunt Margaret, of course. You'll love Margaret. And if my grandmother hasn't other plans, we'll invite her too. Did you know I was named after my grandmother?"

The nurse stroked away the worry mark that appeared suddenly between the patient's eyebrows. She whispered, "Hush now. Breathe in and out, in and out, that's it. Good girl, Miss Earhart. You're doing just fine. I'll tell you when it's over. Then we'll go and meet your grandmother. I can't wait."

* * *

Dorothy Binney Putnam, formerly Dorothy Binney, had never been blissfully unaware. She had always prided herself on being practical, even about matters of the heart. Back when Amelia had stayed at the Rye house, Dorothy had looked out the kitchen window one afternoon and caught her husband giving their guest a ride in the wheelbarrow. George and the aviatrix had bounced along on the lawn, giddy and peppy and gay. In that moment with Amelia, he'd looked ten years younger, Dorothy had felt ten years older, and then and there, she'd known their marriage was over. Still, it would take several more years for the union to disintegrate completely. She'd wanted the boys to be a little older. She'd wanted time to decide which things she would need to hold onto, and which she'd be willing to let go. She wanted time to consider what would become of her.

Some divorcees insist on putting the past behind them. Dorothy wanted no such thing. She was fond of her memories. It gave her pleasure to remember how eager George had been at the outset of their relationship, how he'd pursued her ardently, and how he'd seemed to know details of her life even before she'd told him. He'd been particularly knowledgeable about her father, a genius who'd built an entire empire out of a box of crayons.

When Dorothy had met George, she'd been a freshly minted Vassar graduate, only twenty-three, and full of bold opinions. He'd been a young reporter committed to making a name for himself in politics. With two headstrong personalities, you'd think there would be fireworks, something smashing and euphoric. Maybe there had been on George's end. For Dorothy, however, the relationship began mildly and remained that way ever after. However good-looking and sharp George was, and he *was*, she'd never once felt her heart leap or plunge. When a letter arrived from him, she didn't fawn over the shape of her name in his scrawl. She didn't tear open the envelope like a war bride starved for information. There were no countless wardrobe changes before he came to take her out, no worry that her lipstick might smear onto her teeth, or that he would figure out she'd stuffed her brassiere. Still, she was not against his wooing. He was a solid choice for a husband: ambitious and articulate, with a knack for good timing and for predicting the next zeitgeist. Dorothy liked these attributes. G.P. could hold his own with her and anyone else. She probably wouldn't have married him if he hadn't been so persistent, yet G.P. had wheedled his way into her affections like a cute, wriggling puppy. She'd said, "Very well, I suppose, George," exactly like that, when he'd proposed.

Maybe Dorothy was too accommodating. Maybe that was why she didn't blame A.E. for the dissolution of her marriage. Her friends thought she should, and they called the aviatrix all the h-words—harlot, husband-stealer, hussy, hellcat—but Dorothy knew that A.E. was patently none of these things. The blame fell on G.P., who loved his career and who to a large extent had become his career, at the loss of being a reliable presence in his own family. Dorothy was to blame, also, for not putting an end to that wheelbarrow ride straight away, and for her own wandering eye. Another man, who also happened to be named George, had her up at night, her rose-dotted night-gown damp with frenzied, sweaty emotion. Although this second George was almost twenty years her junior and engaged to boot, she met him whenever she could. When meeting was impossible, she wrote about him in her journal, ardently, and secreted away her journal with even more passion. She supposed she couldn't castigate her husband for having an affair when she was having one too.

So she was to blame, and so was her spouse, but why exempt Amelia? Dorothy Binney Putnam, formerly Dorothy Binney—who, by the end of her life, would be Dorothy Binney Putnam Upton Blanding Palmer—had asked herself this question, and didn't have a ready answer. A.E. was not benign. She was culpable. She was the other woman. And yet, Dorothy recalled the slugs and the ridiculous burial for the cat and the nights she met Amelia in their slippers in the kitchen at half past two in the morning for impromptu graham cracker and chocolate sandwiches, how they told stories and stuffed their mouths until they felt sick, like carefree gleeful children, and she could not bring herself to hold a grudge.

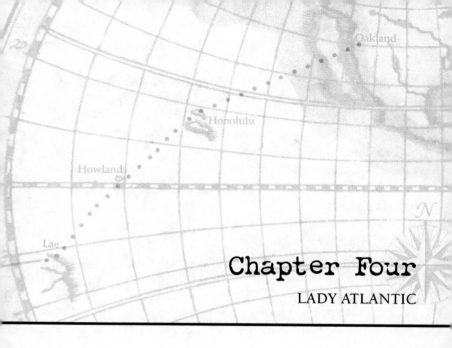

Chapter Four

LADY ATLANTIC

A.E. WAS LOAFING AROUND ON THE SHAGGY WOOL RUG IN the living room. The house in Rye felt especially warm and cozy, with a snow falling into soft hills and gullies beyond the windows, and a cedar fire crackling in front of her. George's son, David, seventeen, insisted that A.E. listen to his favorite new record. A.E. had heard it so many times that evening that when the phonograph skipped, she could sing the lost lyrics.

She was stretched out on her back, a pillow bunched under her feet. Her hands clenched David's open chemistry book, which she held mid-air. She was quizzing him on the periodic table, which he had to memorize before the start of his freshman year at Brown University. She promised that she would remember one element for his every three.

Every so often they would take breaks to eat cold pork chops and potatoes, to see who could do more push-ups, or repeat tongue twisters faster. G.P. sat in an armchair, getting up frequently to answer the phone or to dial it.

"I was thinking about getting a dog," David told her.

Presently, he was sprawled out on a sofa. At six foot four, it scarcely contained him. Legs and arms dangled everywhere like octopus tentacles over the side of a dinghy. He was wearing the prize piece of his wardrobe: a raccoon jacket. Upon receiving his acceptance letter to Brown, he'd insisted on buying it. His reasoning was that all freshmen had one. The coonskin cap on his head, on the other hand, was more Davy Crockett than proud collegian.

"Hmm…what kind?" she asked.

"I dunno. Any old mutt would do, as long as it's friendly and doesn't mind scraps from the commons."

"So you'll you take him with you to college?"

"I suppose."

"You'd better think it through, Davy-boy. A dog's a big responsibility. Maybe a hamster would suit you better. Or a snake."

"Yes, a snake! That would win me admirers, wouldn't you think?"

"Umm, it depends. Are you contemplating a king cobra or a garter snake?"

"Unless you fly to India and swipe a cobra there, I suppose a garter snake. Say, Amelia, where would I find it?"

"I used to catch them outside when I was a girl. I'd take them inside and put them in the breadbox. It drove my mother crazy."

"All you better be getting in college are good grades," G.P. piped in. Having been asked to leave a second boarding school for pranks and generally irascible behavior, David was currently not in G.P.'s good graces. G.P. couldn't believe Brown had accepted him, and wondered if he'd done a favor or sent a bribe and forgotten about it.

"A goldfish," Amelia whispered.

"Oh, no. That won't do," David said. "I had one. Went belly-up in two days."

She rolled over onto her stomach, elbows on the ground, cupping her chin in her hands. The chemistry book was momentarily forgotten. "I have always wanted a goat," she confessed.

"Really?"

Amelia occasionally said outrageous things, David had learned over several years of observation. Sometimes she was best digested with skepticism. Watching her, he thought, should he ever marry, he'd like his wife to be a little like Amelia. He valued her curiosity, enthusiasm, and lack of pretension. She was the kind of girl who could flop down on a rug and arm wrestle without thinking twice. Then, just when he had her pegged as an incorrigible tomboy, she would dress for a night on the town in an enchanting gown, skinny stylish perfection, and he'd have to reframe her in his mind.

"Yes. They have beautiful eyes. Don't you think?" She wasn't being sarcastic, David realized, happily. "The pupils are diamond-shaped. Maybe, when your father and I are through flying and more settled, I'll get one, and a little barn and a little pasture. Someday. Right now I wouldn't be a very reliable care-taker."

"Maybe I'll get *you* a goldfish."

A.E. smiled. "Why don't you give me your jacket and we'll call it a draw?"

David wriggled out of the raccoon coat and tossed it to her.

"Will you get me a hot chocolate? With whipped cream? Pretty please?" she called out to G.P.

G.P. transferred the request to the maid. "Sabine, will you get Amelia a hot chocolate, please? And a coffee for me?"

"And marshmallows, for toasting at the fireplace," A.E. said. "David and I will fetch more kindling from outside."

"And marshmallows, Sabine," G.P. yelled.

"Really, dear, I could have done that myself," she muttered, but he was already back on the phone, complaining to a printer about uneven margins, barking about "professionalism" and "standards."

A.E. turned onto her back again, game for another stab at the periodic table. David groaned.

"Si?"

"Silicon

"Atomic number of Silicon?"

"14."

"Atomic weight?"

"I haven't the slightest."

"Valence?"

"What the deuce is a 'valence?'" he asked.

A.E. wrinkled her nose. "Would you hold it against me if I told you I don't know?"

"A city in France," G.P. called out.

David gave her a capering smile.

"I'm thinking of taking flying lessons," he confessed.

"Where, and with whom? And what is Au?"

"Gold. My old chum, Johnny Finch—do you remember him?—he knows this guy Jackie Fitzwater who lives in Tucson. This Fitzwater is taking on new students, for cheap. Maybe I'll go out there this summer and give flying a whirl. With your blessings, of course."

"I know Jackie. He's okay. But he can talk until the paint dries. And the second coat too."

"Until the cows come home?"

"That's right. Or the goats," she said. "David, I think I'd better introduce you to my friend Paul Mantz. He's the best for flying lessons. I've learned a world from him. If you're willing to drive to California instead of Arizona in the summer, I know he'll take you on."

"Splendid! Don't forget, though, because I've had my eye on lessons for a year now."

"I won't. You'll like Mantz. You'll be chums in no time. Oh, and I've got a book for you. That aerodynamics volume I told you about."

"Great. Show me!"

A.E. frowned playfully and slammed the chemistry text. She and David took off for the library. After G.P.'s divorce, when Dorothy had left with her share of the books, A.E. had taken the opportunity to make her own additions: careful, thoughtful choices. Now when she looked at the library's rows and rows, she saw as much of her own taste as G.P.'s.

"You rascals—don't forget the kindling," G.P. said in their wake. He was still tethered to the phone, looking at a platter holding marshmallows and steaming mugs at his feet. Funny that he hadn't noticed Sabine come in, or leave.

He cut short the conversation, although he doubted he'd gotten through to that thick-headed printer. It was very possible G.P. would fire him come Monday, or at least put him on probation. There was no excuse for amateur typeset errors. If this numskull weren't a friend of a friend, and thus someone he felt obliged to retain, G.P. would have canned him already. He took one of the mugs and planted himself on an ottoman, facing the fire. He watched the wavy air above the blue embers, and drank half the mug before he realized it was cocoa, not coffee.

Goddamn it, he was distracted lately. Maybe it was because of the satin box in his pocket: a two-carat canary diamond. A respectable, romantic ring, given a gutsy boost by the little sapphires surrounding it. Like a circle of bluebirds around the sun. The ring had reminded him of A.E. at first sight, and he'd bought it immediately, even though the jeweler was a crook.

G.P. had been carrying the darn ring in his vest for two years now. A marriage proposal oughtn't be a biennial affair, he thought, shaking his head. After all this time the square bulge felt like it belonged on his chest, the same way the weight of a watch belonged on his wrist. When A.E. finally accepted the ring—if she ever did—he didn't know if he'd be able to part with it.

G.P. took another gulp of cocoa. He swallowed it gloomily. He hated chocolate.

Kicking off his shoes and tugging off his socks, he pulled the ottoman closer to the fire. The almost unbearable warmth felt wonderful on the soles of his feet. He stared at his toes, trying to wiggle them one by one. He started with the pinkie toe of his left foot and ended with the big toe of his right, counting to six. Six toes for the six times he had already proposed. He ticked them off, one by one, wiggle by wiggle, remembering the details of each attempt: where they'd been, what she'd been wearing, whether he'd gotten down on bended knee (he recalled he'd stopped that nonsense after the fourth time—he was getting too old), and the exact words A.E. had chosen to rebuff him. He had to give her credit for creativity. She never used the same excuse twice. Also, she was clever to include him in her dismissals: "But G.P., oughtn't we concentrate on the new business and economize our energy? You told me only a week ago that we're in the red. We don't even have a logo yet. I'm in charge of public relations, which makes *you* in charge of public relations, and we don't have a logo."

That was her latest response. He couldn't argue with her logic. She was a founding partner of a new airline, and like any fledging business, it needed constant care. She was keenly attuned to occupational urgency, as was he. She worked too hard, as did he. She had pointed out that a wedding was an unnecessary diversion, and bother if she weren't right! A.E. wasn't like Dorothy: whimsical, unreliable, happy just to be a hostess.

And yet, it was because A.E. didn't give a darn that he most desperately wanted her to. He longed for the girl she'd been when they met. Then, she'd followed his lead on all matters. She'd taken him at face value. *Live in my house. Work on the book*

I'll publish on your behalf. Go to this press event wearing that dress. "Yes," "yes," and "yes," she'd said. Now he couldn't get her to say "yes" if his life depended on it.

Although he was vain, he didn't delude himself into thinking that she'd ever been submissive to him, or god forbid, reverent. But he did believe that she'd looked up to him, just a little. She'd had enough sense, at least, to see that he was an effective marketer. The marionettes moved when he worked the strings. The troops marched. The monkeys ate their bananas.

After the honeymoon of their acquaintance, though, she'd started to ask questions, good questions. He sounded like a dilettante to his own ears. The seesaw of neediness tilted, and he was ass in the air. But that wasn't his biggest problem. It was the fact that she'd gone from charming neophyte to even more charming idol. The public knew his name, sure. They'd known it for years. But it knew A.E.'s name and face and dress size and hairdo and smile and signature. Why, Clark Gable had been a tongue-tied, stuttering mess when he'd met her. Gable!

With only five minutes to collect herself, A.E. commanded any stage. She gave lectures that made seasoned speechwriters green. With efficient panache, she recycled what she'd said for the weeklies. Emblazoned with her image, newspapers, books, and magazines sold themselves. She upped her appearance fees, commanding as much as movie stars, sometimes more, for an hour's worth of appetizers and chitchat. Whereas she had once accepted all the product endorsements he could scrounge up, she'd become choosier. She refused the "undignified" and "ridiculous" now, and flung those words, like stones, at him. Clearly, she needed no overseer, having broken all kind of records, for altitude, for speed, for anything and everything related to aeronautics. But still she kept him on, out of pity, convenience, organizational necessity, or maybe, if he were very lucky, affection.

He was running out of toes to count. A.E., however, did not seem to be running out of excuses. He felt for the engagement ring, its familiar boxy bulk, in the warmth of his pocket. He considered flinging it into the fire, but couldn't go through with it. He had to find some way of justifying the jeweler's obscene asking price. Maybe the seventh time would be the charm.

The din of laughter from the library gave him hope. The marshmallows still sitting on the tray did too. His odds weren't good, admittedly. But all creatures of flight have to perch eventually. He just hoped he'd be there with a net.

*　*　*

On March 4, 1933, G.P. and A.E. were invited to the Presidential inauguration of Franklin Delano Roosevelt. A.E. was not then, or ever, star-struck around the President or his wife, but that didn't mean she wasn't crazy about them. She saw Eleanor often, and counted her in her circle of closest friends.

Sometimes A.E. traveled with Eleanor to stump for the Democratic party. And sometimes Eleanor traveled with A.E. on her lecture circuit, where she would introduce the aviatrix with a flurry of wildly enthusiastic adjectives. Offstage, the two women could gab about anything. They were instantly and effortlessly comfortable around one another, as if they'd grown up on the same block. They even looked a little alike: both tall and long-fingered, with gold-flecked hair. Their quirks were similar too: A.E. was painfully conscious of her gap teeth, Eleanor of her overbite. Of the two, A.E. was the undisputed beauty, however, at least as Eleanor saw it. Sometimes, gazing at the aviatrix, she had the feeling that she was seeing herself, only stripped of vexing imperfections. The outer corners of her eyes no longer tipped down, woeful like a basset hound's. Her chin was firm rather than jowly.

The two women talked little about their histories. If they had, they would have found even more in common: doting, alcoholic fathers, and mothers who regretted their decision to marry them; backgrounds of power and affluence mixed with the lingering tarnish of bad times; a preference for letters over telephones, and quiet tableside conversations over either. Neither knew of any other woman who had traveled to all seven continents, or who got chills of excitement over a beautifully worded piece of legislation.

G.P. viewed the bond between his protégé and the first lady as a plump maraschino cherry on top of a perfect sundae. He often pressed A.E. to visit Eleanor. He tried to dictate when and where. Once, he finagled a press event around the two women in party dresses, flying a new-fangled, twin-engine Curtiss Condor. Eleanor manned the controls long enough for a round of photos.

"How do you feel, Mrs. President?" a reporter asked.

"Safe. Do you know why? A girl is flying the ship!"

Influenced by her friend, the First Lady recognized the potential of commercial aviation as an industry. She shared the aviatrix's vision of commonplace air travel: a railway of the sky. And she trusted that female pilots were as capable as any other—why not, when she felt as comfortable flying with Amelia as she did driving with most men. Sometimes at night, with the President, she would inquire about various aviation laws and ordinances. Franklin was fond of Amelia too. Nevertheless, he drew the line at this kind of personal prodding.

If he had been paying more attention, he might have noticed that Eleanor couldn't get enough of not only Amelia, but also of flying. She'd been gazing at clouds. She'd been watching birds and butterflies. She'd summoned the physician for a full physical examination: the first step in obtaining a student pilot license. She'd even asked the aviatrix for private lessons. A.E. agreed, so long as she received a basket of muffins as compensation.

"Blueberry, or we're off," she wrote in a letter.

They went up when A.E. visited Washington. Eleanor made up all kinds of excuses in order to slip out of the White House, alone—no easy feat. A.E. insisted on clear days; at the first sign of rain, the aviatrix would call off the lesson.

"I won't endanger the most important woman in America," A.E. explained.

"The second most important, my dear."

The thunderstorm on Eleanor's third lesson caught both women unawares. Gray clouds devoured the sun in an instant. The rain fell noisily, pelting the plane's shell. Frightening rumbles of thunder filled Eleanor's ears, lashes of lightning whipping through space. This is what the journey to Hades must look like: she choked on the thought, unable, unwilling to believe that such a change were possible, that she and her friend had been but blithe, giggling girls a moment ago and now were in true peril. She gripped the aviatrix's arm, squeaking, "Higher, Amelia! Up, up, please."

The aviatrix had never liked to be told what to do, yet the desperation in her friend's voice hastened immediate, unquestioning action. Up they went, sharply, roughly, the clatter of metal all around, the rusty taste of it in their mouths. The sky went navy-black. The color of coffin lining, Eleanor thought. The controls shook in A.E.'s fingers. She felt the shudder of the vessel in her own body.

When she couldn't hold steady any longer, she closed her eyes, for three seconds exactly, counting in her head, her friend's fingers a cold vice on her arm. At three she looked again. A thin lavender light caressed the cockpit windows. The plane stopped shaking. The shrill winds began to subside, the rain to soften. Sunlight burst through holes in the clouds, pale and strong and still. And though the aviatrix had seen a thousand skies, she had to admit that this was one of the loveliest. She glanced at Eleanor. Shocked that she'd made it through, the First Lady leaned over and kissed her.

Exactly one week later she would tell the President that she'd made a decision: she was going to earn her pilot's license. She wanted to join the Ninety-Nines.

"Then, woman, you're going to have to buy your own plane," he replied.

With a guilty conscious, in more ways than one, she sent her new pilot's permit to A.E. With it went a basket of blueberry muffins. The accompanying note read: "Not now, darling, but never say never."

* * *

A.E. regrets that G.P.'s marriage is over. A marriage that's lasted nearly twenty years and produced two children should be harder to toss away, she's said. Yet G.P. and Dorothy are not in love. In the years she has known them, she's seen little in the way of contrary evidence. Though A.E. doesn't want to dwell on what role, if any, she's played in the untwining of hearts, she has to. The press is hounding her. They're convinced she and G.P. will get hitched now that Dorothy's made him a free man. Even A.E.'s friends say it's only a matter of time. They raise their eyebrow skeptically when she insists that he's only her publisher, only her friend, only her manager. Always, an only.

"Methinks the lady doth protest too much," a Ninety-Niner says straight to her face.

Her friends have a point. But she persists with the cat-and-mouse game. The last thing she wants is to purposely hold her personal life up to scrutiny. Her career notwithstanding, she's not sure what she feels or wants these days. The landscape is shifting under her feet, and under G.P.'s too. He's broken off not just with his wife, but with his own publishing company, fed up with the way it's withered over the years, with the greed of certain clients. Following the death of the company's president, he pulls out, selling all his shares to his cousin.

Maybe it's the shakeup that's made him needy. He's more emotional than A.E.'s ever seen him. He starts arguments for no good reason and gets upset when he thinks she's not listening carefully. At night, he insists on holding her very tightly, whereas in the past he's rolled over and cocooned himself in a sheet. And now this—the most disturbing episode: he invites her to his mother's house for what is supposed to be a relaxing afternoon, then ambushes her with reporters, and a marriage license in need of a signature. When she flees in horror, he yells, "It's bound to happen sooner or later!"

Frankly, she's not sure what to do with him. By now, he's become a part of her, somewhere between a vital and vestigial organ, sometimes wholly necessary, other times a nostalgic remnant of her past. He's an essential catalyst in the smooth-running, efficient machinery of her career. Because her life is her career, she can't see herself apart from him. But she can't swear this will always be so.

In truth, his voice in her ear is starting to sound a little like a nuisance. At events, when he insists on continuing to feed her lines, she snaps that she's quite all right, thank you very much. She remembers all the tricks he taught her: don't wear large-brimmed hats, don't lower your voice at the end of a sentence, don't stand pigeon-toed, don't turn your back on an audience, don't dangle your arms at your sides like sausages, don't let your speeches wander. End events crisply and decisively. She thinks of this last point often, and how it pertains to all things in life. With G.P., it could be applicable, too. She outgrew the need for a manager some time ago. She needs, now, a dedicated and fastidious assistant, but she's not sure that G.P. will tolerate the demotion.

During more romantic interludes, she acknowledges that he knows her very well, better than anyone, probably. He must know, then, that she doesn't want to marry. This is how she starts the loathsome letter to him. He's reading it now inside his Rye office, and she's standing outside the door. She's not sure how he'll react, but she's a wreck, her cheeks aflame, her fingers nervously tracing the wavy pattern of the wallpaper. Her weight feels flimsy on her own legs. She rewrote the letter several times before handing over the final draft, but isn't sure this version is any kinder than the first.

> *You must know again my reluctance to marry, my feeling that I shatter thereby chances in work which mean much to me. I feel the move just now as foolish as anything I could do. I know there may be compensations, but have no heart to look ahead.*
>
> *On our life together I want you to understand I shall not hold you to any medieval code of faithfulness to me, nor shall I consider myself bound to you similarly. If we can be honest I think the difficulties which arise may best be avoided should you or I become interested deeply (or in passing) with anyone else.*
>
> *Please let us not interfere with the other's work or play, nor let the world see our private joys or disagreements. In this connection I may have to keep some place where I can go to be myself now and then, for I cannot guarantee to endure at all times the confinement of even an attractive cage.*
>
> *I must exact a cruel promise, and that is you will let me go in a year if we find no happiness together.*
>
> *I will try to do my best in every way and give you that part of me you know and seem to want.*

She has trouble closing the letter. All the usual salutations seem fraught. She chooses finally, A.E., just A.E.

He makes her dawdle a full hour before emerging, but at least he doesn't wreak of alcohol: the smell she most closely associates with brooding men. When she sees him, she buckles. Nearly as tall as G.P., she is hardly the stereotypical little woman falling haplessly into her lover. She is more of a toppled pillar, leaning against one of identical equilibrium.

"That is just about the most unromantic thing I've ever read," he says into her hair. She's sniffling and smiling in spite of everything and wondering how to say what's in her head so it doesn't sound so horrible.

"I think—no—I'm sure, that flying will always come first."

"Obviously."

"Even before family. . .before children. I'm sorry."

The sputtering that comes next is her own blubbering, not G.P.'s horrified, gasping response. There's a long fretful pause and then he says, "Come outside, I have something for you."

She straightens up, assessing him shrewdly.

"No reporters: scout's honor."

Giving him the benefit of the doubt, she slips her arm through his. They walk through the house, with its luxurious rooms and winding corridors, to the backyard. Her eyes are downcast so she sees it immediately, in full force: an enormous parachute pinned to the ground, as if G.P. were a lepidopterist, and this his grandest specimen.

It's mammoth, simply the biggest chute she's ever seen, as outsized in color as it is in dimension: a ripe melon hue with a lime border. G.P. is watching her expression, telling her it's the best parachute they make, twice the standard dimensions for a single-man unit, special-ordered and hand-stitched with loving care by a manufacturer in Quebec. Stretched out on the grass, it seems to want to hover up on its own. Little air pockets bubble beneath the silk. They travel this way and that, finding their way out randomly along the periphery, which is weighted down with garden stones. The parachute reminds A.E. of a planet: a strange two-dimensional planet that quivers and breathes. She thinks, nothing on earth has been as sublime as what she's seen in the sky, until now.

"I've given up on the ring," G.P. says matter-of-factly. "Figure I'll get you something useful."

He takes off his glasses and squints at the tremulous sphere on his lawn, pleased that she is again propped against him, that he has momentarily thrown her off guard.

* * *

G.P. says it again and again: you have nothing to prove. On intellectual, rational, and practical levels she can agree with this. Since crossing the Atlantic as a passenger, she has made tremendous progress as a pilot. The silver wings she pins to her breast, a gift from the U.S. Air Service, she now wears in good conscience. Flying is no longer her pastime. It is what she does. It is who she is.

She has nothing to prove, to her fans or to G.P. or to the press. (Even though, for the last, she knows she is only as good as her last big record.) Still, it would be wasteful to rest on her laurels. Her mother and sister tell her to slow down, why not enjoy the good life for a while. But what is the good life, exactly, Amelia wants to know. She has no desire to lie in a cabana every weekend, or to sip Cabernet day in and day out. She wants to be the one who creates art, change, beauty, not the one who passively observes it. The challenges dangle all around her: irresistibly juicy, ripe, heavy with their own promise. Before anyone else, she yearns to pick them off.

Amy and Muriel and quite a few of her close friends believe that G.P. is her Svengali. Surely he was the one to make the audacious suggestion: that she fly solo across the Atlantic. She has trouble convincing those who love her that the decision is her own. In the three years since the voyage of the Friendship, she has not for a day forgotten the indignity of passing for something she's not. She's been stewing and mulling and brooding, and at last, with the distilled clarity that comes with time, she has made her choice.

She'll have a better plane, one that's worthy of the Atlantic's might. Even so, she gives herself one chance in ten. These odds, if not good, are realistic. Charles Lindberg is still the only person, male or female, to have successfully vanquished that ocean without assistance. In trying to replicate his success, twenty have perished. Not a few planes crashed unobserved, their final resting places now unknown, fodder for seamen's legends. Amelia imagines how the vessels must look, tinseled in kelp, crawling with snails, at the bottom of Lady Atlantic. By now sloshing salt water would have scrubbed off the paint, and fishes would poke in and out of the rust holes, maybe in and out of skeletons too. These images do not fill her with horror, but with a somber pragmatism and acceptance. When she does die, she'd rather be in her plane anyway. She'd like to go quickly, in a spiraling aerial swoon.

She writes a new version of her will and signs it crisply at the bottom. She pays a few small debts and puts sure her affairs in order. She informs G.P. with the assurance of one who has made peace with every outcome, even the unsavory.

"You have nothing to prove," he says. Understanding the futility of this phrase, he adds: "Can't you at least take a navigator?"

"I don't need one. My target is a continent. A blind man wouldn't miss it."

G.P. loves this about Amelia: in the face of doom or success, she maintains a dry wit. He also knows that, with or without him, she will proceed. He has two choices: go along with the Atlantic scheme and market it to high heaven, or find the nearest exit. Because he is in love with her, with her knobby knees and stubbornness and adventuresome core, he agrees.

Truth be told, he's thought about the idea, too. The cogs and wheels in his brain are always churning when it comes to new stunts, and the concept of A.E. soloing the Atlantic has obvious panache. He can't stop her, can't feed her what makes her hungry, so what choice does he have, really, except to support her the best he can. In the harried weeks that follow, as he mechanically places calls and marks off a long checklist, he thinks of ways to woo the press. A.E. should depart on a date that coincides with some other triumph of flight. The look of the plane must be as bold as the pilot herself: vivacious red, ornamented with stripes of black and gold. He'll make the announcement only after she's in the air, to get the reporters panting.

At the Rye house he's sitting at his desk, the to-do list in front of him, a pen in his mouth. He's got the phone pressed to his ear when Amelia leans over his shoulder and whispers, "Gutsy, good-hearted, given to cravings for cherry turnovers at 10,000 feet."

"What are you talking about?"

"Suggestions for my obituary. Do you like the alliteration? It's a nice effect."

He hangs up the phone, killing the voice that's in mid-sentence. He rubs his face with both hands. He tells her he's going to bed. Amelia is her usual self, but the closer they get to take-off, the more terrible he feels.

Amelia takes off the wedding ring she finally accepted from G.P. In the sky she's married to no one. She does, however, pin on her silver pilot's wings. It's become her habit to fly with them always, either tacked on her clothes or tucked in her pocket. She packs her bag: a flying suit from her own fashion line, comb and toothbrush, two scarves, mints, tomato juice in a can and soup in a thermos. With the packing done, she can focus on larger things. The trip calls for an expensive and mostly experimental technical overhaul. Her mechanics have shortened the Vegas's exhaust stacks, replaced the engine with a perky Pratt & Whitney Wasp, and added compasses and a drift indicator. For the plane to cross so many miles, its fuselage must be augmented, and back-up fuel tanks added to the wings. With extravagant tinkering the Vega is granted a 420-gallon fuel capacity and a flying range of 3200 miles. Still, the mechanics are worried. They don't have a rulebook—they're writing it as they go, and they wish their guinea pig weren't a woman. A.E. wants to do the shakedown flights herself, alone, but they insist on coming along. She and the mechanics simulate the weight of the extra fuel with sandbags, flying over New York and New Jersey, jerking and lurching and floundering, dropping the bags as they go, muttering, "Please, Lord Jesus, bless us and don't let us hit anyone."

It's not going to be easy, but she gets the technical go-ahead, finally, and now all she has to do is wait for the weather to cooperate. Every day for over a month she carries her bag to the car and drives thirty minutes from Rye to Teterboro. Every day for over a month she is told to go home. There's too much fog. The rain is impenetrable. The cumulous clouds are thick and hard as banks of ice.

The passing days do not derail her or make her second guess her decision. She yearns for the taste of thin air at high altitude, for the bite of cold through her flying suit. She worries someone else will beat her to the punch. A friend, the pilot Ruth Nichols, tells her she intends to cross the Atlantic before the year is out. Ruth is nimble. and she's a gambler, but she's no fool. Amelia wonders which of them will have grayer hair by the time the weather turns fair.

On May 19th, A.E.'s weather advisor, Doc Kimball, gives a tepid go-ahead. That's all she needs. She grabs some sleep as a colleague flies her to St. John, New Brunswick, and later, to Harbor Grace, Newfoundland. On May 20, exactly three years to the day after Charles Lindberg's ballyhooed crossing, she's off, by herself, her mechanics crossing their fingers and saying more prayers, and G.P. pitching the story far and wide.

The decent weather as far as Newfoundland has given her hope that her solo flight will be less treacherous than it has been for others. She touches the winged U.S. Air Service pin on her heart for luck. It doesn't last long. A storm comes barreling along within hours, erasing her visibility utterly. She's flying blind: the clouds are like billows of the darkest, foulest factory smoke; she can't even see the plane's nose. The moon, which had been providing neighborly comfort, disappears. She uses the scarf around her neck to swab her eyes, which are running from the bite of freezing air, the reek of burning gasoline.

People sometimes ask her what she thinks about at critical times like this one. Usually she'll smile and tell them the truth: it's indulgent to think at all. If she's going to get herself out of trouble, like any good pilot she must think of her plane, not herself. She can't for a second separate flesh from steel, arms from wings, feet from the rudder pedals, hands from the controls. Wisdom is a fine ally, sure, but instinct is the one that counts. In a pinch, instinct will save her life.

The storm is raging outside of her flying machine, thousands of feet above the earth, where the oxygen is precious, and she has to breathe very deeply to keep sound of mind. She descends slightly, but suspects the altimeter is stuck. She's tilted, the plane is angled downward; she can feel the decline. Still, the altimeter registers nothing. She dives lower: the read holds steady at twelve thousand feet. She must be at ten thousand, or even eight thousand by now. Her ears pop like explosive corks, the pressure feels like rocks in her skull. The storm is relentless: it bangs at the wings, pings the tin with hail, and leaves icy hieroglyphics on the windows.

Though she was hoping to swoop under the storm, the lower she gets, the more lethal it seems. She doesn't know exactly how shallow she's flying, but she recognizes she's in a deeper jam than before. She must skirt over the storm instead. Though a higher altitude will eat up her fuel, she has no choice—it's that or continuous physical battery. Ignoring the busted altimeter, she noses up. She passes into and through the worst of the downpour and lightning, holding tight, the whole craft vibrating, and she, at its heart, trembling too. Blood starts to pour out of one of her nostrils. She's hardly aware of this additional unpleasantness. She licks her lips, tasting the warm, brackish-oily fluid with her tongue.

The plane rebels against this new, lofty height. The tachometer, an instrument that gauges the engine's rotational performance, spins crazily. A.E. can now estimate neither her altitude nor her speed, and thus has no sense of how far she's traveled, or even whether she's on course. Nothing is going right, but this is something she has to accept. It's always been one of the possibilities: the complete and utter breakdown of mechanical aid. She makes herself pause between each breath, to keep from hyperventilating, to stave off the terror.

She has no safe haven. At lower levels the storm continues to rage, but the higher she flies, the more weak and debilitated her vessel becomes. For hours she rides an altitudinous roller coaster. She chooses one battle or the other: a collision with squalls and monstrous winds, or the brutal symptoms of mechanical hypothermia, one or the other, over and over, roll the dice and pick your demon.

At the edge of one storm is the beginning of a new, equally vicious one. It tosses the plane, and A.E. along with it. Her hands tense on the controls, and her eyes, though wet and itchy and pink-raw, fasten keenly to the changing sky, hoping for signs of a clearing. She tries to relax the tense muscles in her back; she stretches one leg as far as the compartment's confines will allow, then the other. One of her knees locks. She forces it into reanimation with a stiff, swift chop of the hand. She's been flying for eleven and a half hours now, the whirring motors so loud her ears have given up ringing. She's coping with contaminated, stale air, a cockpit that barely contains her gangly limbs, and a dozen other evils she doesn't dare dwell on. She hasn't heard a human voice for what feels like years, though the radio is on; she wishes someone would talk to her. Cramps roll through her stomach, and probably she should drink some of the soup, but her bladder is full and tight already. Male pilots can use the relief tubes, but these are of no use to women. She's conditioned herself to holding her urine, normally. Considering the situation—probably the worst it's ever been, the closest she's come to perishing—she lets herself pee. The warm release of wet between her legs, which would ordinarily offend her sensibilities, feels oddly soothing.

All she knows is how long she's been flying—there is no other information available to her—but this is enough for her to understand one thing: she's past the point of safe return. She will either make her goal, or not, but she doesn't have enough fuel to return to the airfield at Harbor Grace. If she were driving an automobile, she would pull over now, and rest. A single person in a plane does not have this option, but nonetheless she has to calm herself. With one hand she manages to prick a can of tomato juice with an ice pick she keeps stowed under her seat. She drinks the whole cold can in one go.

The juice gives her the little burst of energy she needs to face the latest crisis: a weld on her manifold shows a visible crack. This means that her fuel is probably leaking out, and she's already wasted so much of it coping with the storms. In addition, carbon dioxide from the exhaust flames is entering directly into the cockpit. No wonder she's having more trouble breathing than usual. Underneath, at a queer angle below her feet, she can actually see the fire from the manifold. With so much to contend with, it's possible the fracture has escaped her attention for a while. The pain in her gut intensifies. Several times she swallows vomit as it spurts up her throat. Unraveling the scarf from her neck, she stuffs it into the crack.

She's much too high, above an altitude any rational mechanic or pilot would approve of, but the Atlantic has so far demanded the impossible. Her plane gives out first. So much ice has formed on the wings it loses its balance, careening down, now in a full-fledged tailspin. The ship nosedives so fast A.E.'s head flings back violently on the divider between cockpit and fuselage, giving her a lump the size of a robin's egg. She can't get the bird under control, it's abused and angry, and now the ocean's surface is visible, terrifyingly so, yet somehow in the knick of time she levels the craft, and coaxes it back up.

Her nose has stopped bleeding, she thinks. Alas, as she feels the bump on the back of her head, she also feels something oozy and slick in her hair. Maybe it's sweat or blood, but more likely it's fuel, and sure enough, when she brings her fingers to her nose to sniff, she realizes it's gasoline dripping from a reserve fuel tank. Glancing at the fuel gauge, she sees it's met the same fate as the altimeter and tachometer. All her equipment: broken, useless. She has her estimation abilities, and faith, and that's about it.

She thinks she will perish. Her odds, not too good to begin with, are much worse now. Even when the sky finally clears and the sight of vivid blue sky and calm soft clouds seems like the face of God himself, she is fairly certain she will die due to insufficient fuel. Or maybe the manifold will be her fiery undoing. It's not until she spots a fishing vessel that she gives herself a decent shot at surviving. A fishing boat, like gulls, means that land is close. The shoreline of which country, she doesn't know, nor does she really care at this point. Originally she'd hoped to make it to Paris, but that feels like a farce.

An hour later she sees the rich textured glory of coastline, lush greens and savory browns, and she laughs out loud. Descending, she sees railroad tracks and a meadow, but no airfield, and so settles on a grassy pasture that looks level enough. The landing takes every last iota of her concentration, and the plane's stamina. "Please don't catch fire, please don't catch fire," she says, as wheels meet land. Upon impact, the injured manifold might detonate the whole craft. She opens the hatch and gets out of the plane quickly, if stiffly. Relieved but not quite convinced she's going to make it, she scurries away from the vessel, which is smoking.

Finally, she settles down in the field quite a ways from her plane. She lies somewhere on the map of the world, a random tiny speck in Scotland or England, maybe even Spain. On her back she just breathes. In another minute she'll change her soiled pants and scrub the grease and crusted blood from her face, the gasoline streaks from the nape of her neck. She'll splash her eyes with water and hope they are not too pink. She'll suck on a mint and run a comb through her hair, and walk quite a ways before finding an astonished, not unkind farmer named Dan McCallion, who will inform her that she is in Londonderry, in the north of Ireland, in the middle of his cow pasture.

In another minute, life will be entirely different, life will be hers again to possess, but for now she is still on the cold earth, grateful for the feel of it on her back, against her calves and buttocks and the back of her head. She stares up at the wide sky that has accommodated her, yet again, and she whispers humbly: "Thank you."

✶ ✶ ✶

The press is mostly kind. This may be G.P.'s handiwork, or maybe the world still has a big appetite for her. She takes the praise with humility. When called "lustrous," "an idol," and "breathtaking," she is diffident. A few outlets accuse her of being vainglorious and reckless, and she figures she must accept these responses too, if she's to accept any.

Why did she do it: that's what they really want to know. She's tried to discern the lure of the air before. It's the lure of beauty, of course, but it's more than that. It's beyond words, beyond grasp, too wide and sacred to get her arms around. She flies because it is her religion, her tonic, because the experience is wretched and beautiful both. It's the end of the human experience and the beginning of what she imagines must be immortality. And yet, this explanation is not nearly enough, and it seems unjust and dishonest to offer it.

Why do you fly, they want to know, from Denmark to South Dakota. Simply, why?

She stalls, coming up with this—a blithe, whimsical line. "I do it for the fun of it." This seems to satisfy them, and keep them quiet for a while.

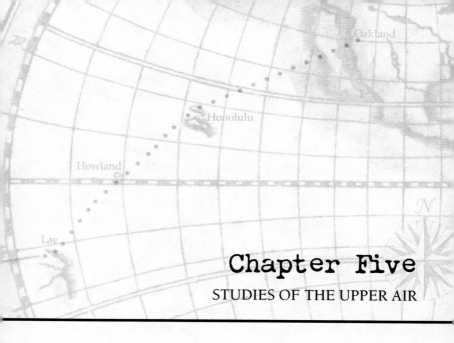

Chapter Five

STUDIES OF THE UPPER AIR

SHE FEELS, IN HER HEART, THAT SHE CAN BE CONTENT ONLY if she does this one last thing. Go around the world, at the widest point: the equator. No one's done it before. There is no greater feat. If she can do this, then she can relax. Perhaps she'll retire and get her little farm and goat, as she'd told David she might do. She will read more books and see more of her friends and travel like a proper person who keeps proper hours in a proper house, suitcases in the closet rather than beside the front door.

If she just gets through this last stunt, she'll have enough money for everything she already has, and probably enough for everything she'll ever want.

For the first time in all the time they've been together, G.P. says "no." He's plainspoken, no spinning or finessing.

She reasons with him as she's reasoned with herself, telling him she's already crossed many of the legs individually: the Atlantic, all of America, from California to Hawaii.

"It's a matter of combining the legs, adding a few more, and selling the whole package for a premium."

"You've spent too much time listening to me, clearly," G.P. replies.

"I know I can do it."

He is moved by her vivaciousness. How could he not be? It's contagious. His wife is the glittery, twinkling star atop the tree of can-do propaganda.

"If it were only your abilities we needed to consider, there would be no question. I'd be the first in line waving bon voyage. But it's not just that. There's the weather, there's the entire African continent, which is basically uncharted; there's the Pacific, no slouch to the Atlantic. I know for a fact that there's a lack of distribution channels for oil and gas in most of Asia. Have I mentioned all the shots you'll have to take? Do you remember how sick you got from the malaria vaccine alone? I could go on."

She sits on the tiled floor of the kitchen in her favorite brown slacks and nods. "Would you, please?"

"In addition, he says, clearing his throat, "there are other human beings you should consider. Me, for one, your husband. I don't want to lose another wife. I've told you before, you're my favorite so far, and I'm fairly convinced I couldn't replace you."

"Well, you're right about that."

"Let's not forget about the future. We've got a comfortable-enough life, haven't we? We could do better, yes, but we could do a helluva lot worse."

"This doesn't sound like you at all."

"I'm getting old, what can I tell you."

"I think I like the younger George."

"I'd rather you leave me for a younger, handsomer bloke than try to make it all the way around the world."

"That's not true."

"Believe me, it's true."

She pauses and fiddles with a stray thread on her hem.

Unsentimentally, she asks, "What would you do without me?"

"Well, for one thing, I'd get a hell of a lot more sleep."

"Seriously."

"I don't know. I don't know what I'd do."

"Well, when I make it, will you manage to forgive me?"

"*If* you make it."

"Okay, if."

"Probably."

"And you'll still love me?"

"Probably," he says gruffly. "Whether I like it or not."

* * *

Her father's cancer is spreading. The news takes Amelia to California immediately. As Amelia imagined it, the cancer is spreading like a rampant exotic flora in the fever of his body. She can envision it clearly: the surrendering of his cells and brittle bones to this invasive species. Externally, she doesn't need her imagination to see the damage wrought. Her once dashing father weighs one hundred and twenty pounds and has trouble moving his hands. He is confined to his bed, a skeleton under blankets. There, Helen, his new wife (well, not so new anymore—A.E. supposes she will always perceive her parents' divorce as recent, and Helen as temporary), hovers dotingly. A.E. pays for some tests and procedures that should have been done a long time ago. On the X-rays, the doctor points to ominous splotches on Edwin's trunk: stomach cancer that's moved to his kidneys and liver. Like a parasitical vine leeching from a compromised host, she thinks. She reads the doctor's grimness. She okays the blood transfusions anyway, though the doctor insinuates it's too late, and gets out her checkbook again. The doctor tells her they can keep fighting, but he'd rather they make her father as comfortable as possible. It's decided by the women in Edwin's life, Amelia and Helen, that morphine is the right option. Less struggle, more mercy. When the drip is in effect, Edwin changes almost instantly. The fear in his big brown eyes flies away. He stops shaking, flapping his arms and groaning. The stricture that has been keeping him from eating loosens up, and he welcomes applesauce and hot chicken soup, spoon-fed. Amelia and Helen treat him like a baby, fitting a bib around his neck and catching dribbles from his lips. Amelia reads to him and tells him stories and listens patiently when he talks. Every few hours she slips outside his house, or into the bathroom, and has a good cry.

★ ★ ★

Muriel calls. She wants Edwin, but would like to talk to her sister first. Helen hands her the receiver of the phone, and kindly, politely, leaves the room. A.E. talks into the mouthpiece quietly.

"Hi, Pidge. How are you? How's mother?"

"I was helping her clean the house and found some of the clothes you made me. Remember how you once cut Mother's old silk curtains from in the attic and sewed our Easter dresses? All winter we looked for empty bottles to redeem so we could buy velvet ribbons. I think that Easter dress was the nicest thing I ever owned."

A.E. is not sure how to take this—whether this is a manipulative call for more clothes or a kind sisterly reminiscence. She decides to give Muriel the benefit of the doubt.

"I remember. Well, I loved to make you things. I loved to make you happy."

"You were always a good big sister. Always caring and responsible, with a better sense of purpose than I have."

"Don't be so hard on yourself."

"At least I have Albert. Even when I'm no good at all, he's still protective of me. He still takes care of me."

A.E. hardly thinks of Albert as an asset, and so says nothing.

"It was just so difficult," Muriel continues. "We were little, too little to know what was happening between Mother and Pa, and I felt caught in the middle. All the bickering, all the stewing and stomping and door-slamming. Oh, how it wore me down! I think you got less of it, being daddy's girl. I'm so proud of you for being with Pa right now. I wish. . .I wish I could be there too, but I can't, I can't, I don't think I could even bear to talk with him! If I hear how weak his voice has gotten I'll start crying."

"No, we can't have that. He needs strength and support right now, not a reminder that he's terribly frail. He's really not in good shape, Pidge. I think it's a matter of days. . .a couple of weeks, at the most."

"Am I a terrible person if I don't talk to him. . .before. . ."

"No, you're not a terrible person." A.E. says resolutely.

Now Muriel is crying full force into the phone and A.E. is sorry for her and embarrassed for her and a little impatient because she can't be taking care of everyone, not all at once. She knows that Muriel, whether by natural deficiency or cultivated indolence, cannot be counted on. She lives to this day in her old familiar role: the sensitive one. The fragile one. The high-strung one.

"I'm sorry, Pidge, I am. It's a terrible thing. Try not to think too much about how he is now. Focus on when he was young and healthy. No one was as charming as Pa in his heyday."

"That's the truth," Muriel says in a whisper. "I think, to this day, Mother's still in love with him. She never got over him."

"Well, how could she? That would be impossible." the aviatrix responds.

★   ★   ★

A.E. stays at her father's residence for days, sorting out

paperwork, preparing his obituary, and contacting his old friends to let them know his time has come. She fakes upbeat telegrams from her sister and mother. She lies to Edwin directly, saying he's won the big legal case he's been worrying over. She wants to be there when he goes, so she waits as the time moves ever more slowly. She feels as if she's a passenger on a crucial flight, with no control, watching the world through side windows. Eventually Helen takes her aside and tells her it's okay to leave, Edwin understands. He's always loved her dearly and always will. Her conscience intact, if not her heart, A.E. bids farewell, deciding, at the end of her father's life that she will proceed with the business of living her own. That's what Edwin wants, Helen says. Within hours of A.E.'s departure, he passes. She's glad that the last expression she saw on his face was everyday bemusement. He'd been watching his wife assemble a puzzle, his eyes flitting from her to the image of the Washington Monument taking shape, little by little.

Now, A.E. can't help but think about her mother's future. She's not sure how much of a role she is supposed to play in Amy's well being, or how far she should bend to appease her. Obviously her mother would prefer that she settle down, preferably nearby, on the East Coast. She has never understood the nomadic tendencies of her elder daughter. But if settling down means shucking one's ambitions and accepting the kind of domestic unrest her sister endures, well then, A.E. cannot make this sacrifice. She will pay for her mother's future needs, that much she can, and will, do. She'll buy a nice house in California, an easy walk to the park and the grocery store and yes, the hospital too. Year-round it's warm out West. There will be citrus trees out back, and a hammock. It will be a real improvement to the ice and perennial gray of Boston, A.E. thinks, signing the mortgage on a house that needs renovating in her name, and Amy's, and creating a joint bank account. For now, she will continue to write to her mother, and visit her when it's convenient. She will not, however, heed Amy's misguided advice. Edwin's death made her long for closer ties to family, but only weeks after his funeral, she's beginning to feel more ambivalent.

The fire in the house at Rye cements her desire to fly around the world. It's the fault of the groundskeeper, says G.P. He went into the basement, turned on the heat in an empty boiler, and never turned it off. G.P. isn't going to sue: there's no point, no money to be made. The fire ravaged a whole wing. Smoke, ash, and water from the fire hoses damaged the rest of the property. The beautiful dining room where she and G.P. had so often entertained is a charred shell. Strips of singed wallpaper flap against the walls at half-mast. The fire has eaten the upholstery on the furniture and blistered the wood. It has charred the oak of the central stairway and banister. It has cracked the cerulean tiling in the front hall. Having shipped those tiles from China specifically for the house, G.P. is stricken. He's always been inordinately fond of them. Once, A.E. caught him on his hands and knees cleaning them in the middle of the night.

Lost in the fire are her favorite photo albums, the strange, beautiful parachute, G.P.'s personal publishing archive, all matters of aeronautical equipment. Gone are boxes of fan mail, newspaper clippings lovingly cut and filed by her mother, a Purple Heart an old man had handed to her with a respectful salute in Dallas, original paintings by Norman Rockwell, patterns from her clothing line, and an assemblage of life-size mannequins she'd used to fit her clothes. Lost in the fire are all the books she purchased for the library.

Gone are sentimental things she should have thrown away: ten skeins of purple yarn and an amateurishly executed blanket, the sled she'd used as a kid, one of The Canary's old wheels which Neta had thought to save for her.

For G.P. the greatest loss is the property itself. For A.E., it's the wooden box on the dining room mantle that contained the first chapter of a never-written novel and the sum total of her life's poems. She'd written hundreds, and stored every one of them there. It was a dream of hers to sit down one afternoon and read them all in one turn. Once G.P. had tried to get his hands on them to create extra content for an article—"filler," he'd said—but she wouldn't let him.

"Private. Mine. Don't touch. *Please.*"

They probably weren't very good, her poems. At least she can imagine that they were. This is the bright side of loss, she decides: the pink, pearly nacre of nostalgia.

Lost, finally, is the sense of home she used to carry around with her. The Rye house was the habitat she felt most comfortable in and the only one she shared with G.P. Now there is no rest stop between their lives, his on the East Coast, hers on the West. Her first inclination, upon hearing of the fire, is to fly back immediately, to comfort him and to share in their grief. G.P. persuades her not to.

"Only one of us should be this queasy," he says.

But A.E. knows the truth, already, and the truth is this: Whether you look for it or not, change will find you.

G.P. is grateful that one item survived the wreckage. He tells her that the case containing her awards is unharmed. She dismisses the importance of this, but G.P. doesn't. He's always admired the case, in part because of the coy way A.E. treats it. He saw her open it only once, when a little boy, visiting the Rye house with his parents, asked to see what was inside. She'd let the boy monkey around with its contents without a second thought. Soon, gold medals were rattling around his neck, blue ribbons were astrewn on the floor. The boy treated the badges and rosettes like playthings, and A.E. in response asked only that he put them away neatly when he was done.

That box, G.P. thinks, that box is the very definition of his wife.

★ ★ ★

Purdue has offered a nice chunk of money for her to live on campus part-time and be a counselor for the female students there. The school administrators are loose in their definition of counselor. They seem to want a role model, a giver of sisterly and motherly advice, and older version of who these girls can become. A.E. packs some things and moves to her on-campus quarters, which is in the girls' dormitory. One by one, the girls knock on her door, pouring out their hearts drop by drop. A.E. encourages them to strive for the best, to use their educations to be doctors instead of nurses, lawyers instead of secretaries. If they are adventurous at heart, to be aviatrixes like her. She tells them to set the bar high in all of their endeavors, and not to waste time lamenting their failures. Pick yourselves up, dust off your knees, and try again, she instructs them.

The girls, though appreciative, do not always see themselves reflected in A.E. In fact, many of them perceive her as an anomaly. Surely America has room for no more than one famous female pilot, and 98 others.

"Hogwash," A.E. insists, more upset than she lets on. "Female pilots have become an everyday phenomenon. Why, one of my dear friends has a regular job as an airmail pilot."

"But how many female airmail pilots are there, in total?" the girls want to know.

"Dozens."

She is lying. Her friend Helen is the only one, but she'll be damned if she'll let the girls win this argument.

The co-eds are also skeptical about how they are to have both families and careers. On this matter A.E. doesn't mince words.

"You have to consider your career *before* you get married. Will you have your own income or have to wait for your husband to give you spending money? Will he help mind the children? If the answer is 'no' to these questions, then, frankly, a career and family are not possible in tandem. Trying to do both is like trying to drive a bus and fly a plane at the same time. Of course, mine is only one voice. Perhaps you will prove me wrong."

A.E. relays these conversations to G.P. on the telephone. He thinks that Purdue should give his wife more, considering how much time, energy, and advice she is providing. Why not shoot for the stars and ask the school for a bigger, better plane? She will need one when she flies around the world.

He puts together a proposal and brings a bottle of cognac to the president of Purdue. President Elliott smiles wearily and puts the cognac on his desk, leaving the red ribbon around its neck intact.

G.P. makes himself at home in the office, taking a seat and stretching out his legs. He tells the president that the cognac is one hundred years old.

"Is that so?"

"I was hoping to see for myself if it aged well." He fishes in his pocket for the corkscrew he brought along.

President Elliott laughs uncomfortably. He is not sure if he admires or is put off by G.P.'s audacity. "I'm afraid I don't have any glasses. I'm a teetotaler at work."

"Not a problem." G.P. clicks open the latch of his briefcase and unearths two tumblers, each wrapped in a white hand-kerchief.

"I see you come prepared!"

"For business, I try. For friends, always," he replies. He's smiling and President Elliott decides he'd better have a chair and inform his secretary that he won't be taking calls right now.

"The thing is," G.P. says, when each man is on his second drink of the cognac that was actually made last year, in a bathtub, and then poured into a good bottle, "Amelia adores Purdue. She's with your girls night and day, tirelessly coaching them on success for females in this brand new world. She'll do anything for your school."

"And we adore her. The girls can't praise her enough. They

are entranced as much by her clothes as by her accomplishments. Trousers! My wife says only Amelia and Katherine Hepburn could pull them off with such élan."

"Just wait, next year all of Purdue's girls will be wearing them." G.P. pulls in his legs and leans forward suddenly. "I hope, though, my wife's service to Purdue has consisted of far more than fashion influence."

"Indeed! The insight, the intellectual stimulation, the avenues she has opened up for these girls are invaluable."

"Invaluable," G.P. repeats, topping off the president's glass. He himself has slowed down. He knows in which bathtub the cognac was conjured, and it was not the cleanest tub in the world. "Yes, but if we had to put a number on the legacy that Amelia is creating here on campus, on the grace and attention she brings, and quite frankly on the sharp increase in highly qualified young women applying to your school, what do you suppose it would be?"

The president brings the glass to his lips. He is not yet drunk, just a little fuzzier, sleepier. He can see where G.P. is steering this conversation. "I'll level with you, George. Your wife's salary is already the equivalent of a tenured professor's. To be honest I've heard some rumblings from faculty members who feel like she's stolen a little of their thunder. Selfish and egotistical that may sound, perhaps, but my job is to maintain equilibrium, peace. I have to ensure that everyone on my campus is content. Money can be divisive, no matter how deserving the recipient."

"Which is why I propose to you the Purdue Research Fund," G.P. says.

"The Purdue Research Fund…"

"Now wait." G.P. waves off the president's cautious echo. "Hear me out. Although you don't know it, The Purdue Research Fund already exists. I just contributed one thousand dollars to it out of my own pocket, in fact. What the fund is, is a nonprofit, nonpartisan mechanism for increasing awareness of aviation science here at Purdue. A.E. is charmed by your school, as I said. She wants to sing its praises to a larger audience and she thinks that the research fund is the way to do it. Since the groundwork has already been laid, we seek not initial operating costs, but capital for growth. A 50-fold match on my recent contribution would ensure the purchase of a scientific research plane that Amelia would personally pilot and supervise. This plane would bolster Purdue's rather, forgive me, shabby aviation offerings, and further, enhance Purdue's biology department."

"The biology department!"

"Yes. You see, the plane will be equipped with first-class air sampling facilities, a flying laboratory, for trekking those bacteria that exist above human occupation, but which might eventually inhabit our own environment. 'Upper Air Studies,' this field is called. Its popularity is increasing. I hear Princeton and Yale and the University of Southern California have already invested big money. They're projecting it will become their most lucrative area of science. Princeton has been pestering me to work with them on the flying laboratory. But considering Amelia's attachment to Purdue, I felt obliged to give you first dibs on the opportunity."

President Elliott happens to know that one of the disgruntled academics of which he spoke is a biology professor. This "Upper Air Studies" sounds a bit ridiculous, but what is academia, in the end, if not an exercise in the ridiculous and promising?

He hesitates, looks at his drink, and looks at the door. It has been shut now for exactly twenty-eight minutes. His secretary knows to phone after thirty. Sorry to interrupt, she'll say, per their pre-arranged protocol, but it's an emergency: a student caught with an illegal substance, an irate parent, a member of the building and zoning committee throwing a tantrum. President Elliott would like G.P. to leave. He really would. But at the same time, there might be value in this "flying laboratory" notion. Elliott envisions this plane of the future: lots of glass and smooth contours, Bunsen burners and simmering chemical concoctions inside, like nothing ever created before.

Well now, he may just have to bow out of the fraudulent emergency. This G.P. fellow may be on to something.

After the better part of the bottle of cognac has been drunk and a week has passed, Elliott and a small group of deep-pocketed alumni subsidize G.P.'s scheme: this so-called Purdue Research Fund. G.P. draws up the contract. The moniker Purdue appears twenty-three times on the document, but sole ownership and custody go to one person and one person only: Amelia Mary Earhart.

This is a feat, even for G.P. He is ebullient for about a half hour, and then thinks he cannot celebrate any longer because there is still so much to do. Onward and upward. He hires a young secretary in Hollywood named Margot, who is at least as enamored of the aviatrix as the most starry-eyed Purdue girl. He also contacts Paul Mantz, A.E.'s longtime affiliate, to be her pre-flight technical consultant. Mantz, who is going through a divorce, declines at first, but G.P. brings up the history he shares with A.E. Mantz holds out a few more minutes, than changes his guilty "no" to a reticent "yes."

G.P. is pleased by these hires. He'll do grunt work if he has to, but he much prefers managing others. He takes special pleasure in watching Margot sort through A.E.'s fan mail: a 50 lb. sack of letters a week, and a half-ton backlog. The secretary shares his pride at the overwhelming support for the aviatrix. Like G.P., she tends to get sappy and sentimental over notes from particularly worshipful fans. Perhaps the biggest admirer is Ceci DeRisio, an eight-year-old girl from New Haven, Connecticut.

"How many letters has she written?" G.P. asks.

"Let me see . . ."

As Margot counts envelopes, she dabs her finger on her tongue. G.P. notices both tongue and nails are the same shade of watermelon pink.

"Fifty-seven read and thirty-four still to be opened. In the last one, Ceci volunteered to be Amelia's on-flight assistant. Isn't that precious? Say, if this little girl hits 100 letters, will she get a prize?"

Margot is joking, but G.P. gives the idea serious consideration. He tries to picture it: human interest story; plucky little girl with ruddy cheeks and sooty hands; she's all but a street urchin, pen and paper her only conduit to the civilized world. It's not bad.

"When your boss returns from her latest foray," G.P. says, "maybe we'll invite Ceci DeRisio to Hollywood."

"Well, *that* would be wonderful," Margot replies.

The other new employee, Mantz, is less enthusiastic. He's all business on the phone with G.P., and it takes longer than G.P. planned for him to produce a list of what the new plane should have.

G.P. takes one look at it and makes slash marks with his pencil.

Mantz writes a shorter list.

G.P. slashes that too.

The next list Mantz hands over has a note in capital letters at the top.

THIS IS THE BARE MINIMUM, GEORGE. I MEAN IT.

Yet what Mantz wants still seems exorbitant. G.P. knows that the longer stretches in the air will call for a higher fuel capacity. But does A.E. really need a specially designed confluence of fuel tanks, ten in all, scattered about the wings and fuselage?

"Yes," Mantz says adamantly. "And the master valve ought

to be moved to the floor of the cockpit."

"Should it be 14 carat gold too?" G.P. wants to ask.

Mantz recommends a Sperry Robot pilot, state-of-the-art Western Electric radio equipment that works in both code and voice, an overhead hatch at the rear of the plane for the navigator, and special orange paint strategically applied to the outside. God forbid the plane goes down, at least it will be easier to spot. The vessel itself should be a seaplane. Traveling at the equator, much of A.E.'s travel will be over the water. It only makes sense, Mantz says—water pontoons instead of wheels. They will be more expensive, but worth the investment in A.E.'s safety.

G.P. investigates these water pontoons and is aghast. They come at a charge of $30,000. Shoot, what next—a parachute that will support the whole of the plane's weight? Mink-trimmed seats? They're overbudget as is. Though Purdue has been generous, the research fund will cover only 75% of the total costs. The rest A.E. and G.P. will have to take from A.E.'s lecture circuit and product endorsements. George may have to sell A.E.'s old plane too. She's not happy about this, but he doesn't see another way. Some months they barely have enough to pay for the houses on both coasts, their travel, and all the people under their employ. Amelia, big-hearted to a fault, is always sending money to her mother, her sister, a half dozen greedy cousins who have crawled out of the woodwork. An additional $30,000—great Jehosophat.

Undaunted, Mantz recommends a Sikorsky S-43 plane— another affront to G.P.'s business sense. A.E. has a longstanding, profitable relationship with the Electra brand. It would be ridiculous to sever it now. No, she must have her Electra, an Electra with wheels.

G.P. tries to break it to Mantz as tactfully as he can. We're in an economical dip. Now's the time to be frugal. G.P. doesn't want to bruise his ego, at least not prematurely. He'll probably still need Mantz's advice and contacts. There's a silence and then Mantz calls him disgraceful and negligent. G.P. lets this go because Mantz has women problems; because he's an airman, and thus by nature unreasonable; and because A.E. will be mad if he utters Mantz's name and "donkey's ass" in the same sentence.

"Paul—how can I make this clear to you? You want me to buy communication equipment that has yet to be invented. You ask me to take precautions against completely inconceivable disasters. You want everything special-ordered and custom-made. If I were a richer man, I'd buy Amelia this dream plane, sure I would. I'd buy myself a yacht too."

G.P. can hear Mantz brooding over the phone. His breathing is heavy and salivary.

"What about the refractory orange paint? Will you at least do that, for Amelia's sake?" Mantz asks.

G.P. fears he will lash out. In a rare moment of altruism triumphing over brusqueness, he holds his tongue. He doesn't divulge that the paint has already been picked: black and gold, Purdue's school colors.

After he's done haggling with Mantz, he's back on the horn with others. He's got permits and licenses to procure, maintenance crews to organize, maps and charts to gather, equipment to be mailed, landing fields to locate, gas depots and housing sites to confirm, interpreters to hire, and weathermen to consult. He's almost out of money by the time he remembers the flying laboratory. To this he allots the last five hundred dollars. He's spent every dime when Mantz calls back to remind him about internal communications on the plane. G.P. looks in the shed at Rye and finds an old bamboo fishing pole. To one end he affixes a clip that can hold written notes. A.E. in the cockpit and her crew in the cabin can pass the pole back and forth, he reasons. It's not an ideal solution, but it's better than nothing.

He's known from the get-go that being A.E.'s publicist

means resourcefulness, thrift, and complete dedication. Trouble is, he's got other jobs and other people to please. He's a got a multi-picture contact with Major Pictures, and if he wants to keep it, he'd better start pulling his weight. In between trying to find the perfect flight goggles for his wife, he thinks of ways to promote *Go West Young Man*, Mae West's new movie. The censors have vetoed his movie posters. They're too racy. West's breasts take up half the space.

His is an odd life, to be sure. But he wouldn't trade it, not for anything, not for massive cleavage on every marquee in America.

* * *

Whilst G.P. plays conductor to this whirligig symphony, A.E. keeps apace. She commutes mercilessly between her student counseling at Purdue, the East Coast to see G.P., and the West Coast, where she brushes up on new flying techniques and supervises renovations of the Hollywood house. The repairs are on schedule and A.E. is pleased to see that the rooms she has been most concerned about, a spacious bed and bath for her mother, look exactly as she hoped they would.

Amy has spent more than enough time in Muriel's household with Muriel's insufferable husband. Lately both her mother and Amy have dropped hints about an impending divorce, a development A.E. would gladly support. A.E. won't believe it's actually happening, however, until her sister hires a lawyer.

Even if the divorce goes through, A.E. would still like Amy to stay with her. She wants her mother to relax, away from the grandchildren she tends to smother with affection. The California home will be a restful place, for mother and elder daughter. A.E. has made sure that Amy's quarters are far from hers—a safeguard.

Squished in the spare margins of an already packed

schedule are still more obligations. A.E. has promised Eleanor she will campaign with her. In addition, A.E. is stomping for the Ninety-Nines, and for her neighbor in Rye, Caroline O'Day, who is running for congresswoman as an incumbent. The aviatrix is surviving on sugar and a severely truncated sleep schedule. She's dismayed but not really surprised when her hair starts falling out. There's a little bald patch behind one ear that she takes pains to hide. Every time she washes her hair, she finds another clump in the drain. The problem with her tongue—this Geographic Tongue—is worse, too. There's a new patch. She swears it's the shape of Africa.

* * *

On a rare free evening A.E. settles into the part of the Hollywood house that has ceiling and walls. The rooms smell like fresh paint and sawdust. She's intent on talking to no one and doing nothing—rest, even if she has to take half a sleeping pill again—but changes her mind when the new girl, Margot, brings her a mug of hot chocolate and a little toy plane.

I made it myself, Margot says shyly. At A.E.'s urging, the girl shows her how she assembled the parts, how the wheels actually roll, where the wood resisted glue and she had to hammer tiny nails. One side of the plane says "Amelia's Attacks!" which makes the aviatrix laugh.

"What a thoughtful girl. Thank you!" she says.

"This is nothing compared to what another one of your fans has done," Margot replies. She's standing and fidgeting and nervous until A.E. tells her to sit down on a chair and be at home.

"Who's that?"

"She's a young girl named Ceci DeRisio. She's written you over a hundred letters. I've counted!"

"A hundred?"

"Yes, almost one a day for the past four months."

"That's a dedicated young lady."

"Mr. Putnam said maybe he would invite her to visit you—when you return from your trip, of course."

A.E. winces. The thought of even one more commitment, however justified, seems excruciating. She and G.P. talk frequently about slowing down, but he still books things without consulting her, and then expects her to jump through every hoop and over every hurdle. It seems all conversations revolve around work, to the point that she no longer feels relaxed or affectionate when she sees him, but tense, ready for his next orders. Most recently he's arranged for her to write a book about her trip around the world. It will be published in installments in *The New York Herald Tribune*. While the deal is surely lucrative, A.E. knows she will have difficulty writing about her trip at the same time that she is experiencing it.

A.E. eats the whipped cream on top of the cocoa with a spoon. Margot is still staring at her brightly, and the aviatrix realizes she has no right to be wallowing. She's far from a pitiable subject. Why, girls like Margot and Ceci DeRisio want to *be* her. In her wildest dreams, she couldn't have predicted such flattery.

"Will you give me one of Ceci's letters? I'd like to read it."

Margot bounces up like a rubber ball. "Oh, it would be my pleasure, Miss Earhart."

Squinting, A.E. reads the letter, tucks it into its envelope, and puts both into her pocket. Margot is beaming.

"It's a lovely note," A.E. acknowledges. She must suppress her full appreciation, or else it will come welling up with embarrassing force.

"Margot, I've been meaning to ask you something. I just bought a new flight jacket and wondered if you'd like my old one? I'd wager this toy plane is worth more, but the jacket's yours if you want it."

Ebullient, Margot struggles to say something, and manages finally to nod.

★ ★ ★

If A.E. speaks cavalierly of the upcoming flight, secretly she is intimidated. The twin-engine Lockheed G.P. has procured is a totally different animal from her old plane. It weighs in at a staggering 15,000 pounds. Though heavy, it's fast, with a cruising speed of 180 miles an hour, and a top speed of 200. Topped off with fuel, the all-metal aircraft is capable of traveling 4000 miles straight. It's a powerful bird, and yet A.E. is not sure she's made a good trade. The onboard instruments, complex and unfamiliar, make her nervous. In fact, some of the switches and gizmos seem downright alien. A.E. tries to concentrate as Mantz explains how they work. He teaches her how to use the Cambridge analyzer, how to achieve maximum mileage by adjusting the fuel mixture control, and how to drop a trailing wire as an adjunct to her radio. The 250-foot wire will enable players on the ground to get a "fix" on her, Mantz says, something that her old system didn't guarantee. Although A.E. watches patiently as he spools out the wire, once they are aloft, she is not impressed. To the aviatrix the wire is simply one more new thing to master. It feels like overkill. She's always preferred to fly with as little equipment as possible.

"Just me and my plane, if you please. No clutter."

Mantz, who is as much a pragmatist as she is a romantic, is appalled when she says this. He tells her she's being irresponsible. She'll need every bit of the new equipment. Moreover, she'd better know it inside and out before the flight.

Mantz urges her to spend more time in the air. He even volunteers to accompany her on a shakedown flight across the country.

"Now that my wife is divorcing me, what else have I got to do?" He tries to play down the importance of the shake-down, but A.E. can see he's genuinely concerned.

"No can do. Sorry, Paul."

Okay, well, what about some extra lessons on the radio? We can do those on the ground, right here in California."

"Oh, I'll be all right."

Maybe because he's got nothing to lose, and A.E. has everything, Mantz presses harder.

"The radio is going to be your lifeline, Earhart. Everyone uses code nowadays and you're still relying on voice. I have to be upfront: your skills are rusty. You'll be lucky if you pass the new radio tests before your flight."

"Now you're just being hard on me," she replies.

"Yeah, for your own good! Code doesn't take long to learn. A quick study like you, you could have it down in a week."

A.E. doesn't like to be pressured. She gets enough of that from her husband. Then and there, she decides not to expend effort arguing with Mantz. When she takes off for the trip of her life, Mantz will still be on the ground. She'll be the one at risk. Thus, she should be the sole decision-maker. If her decisions end up to be poor ones, well, she will take responsibility for them. She's always preferred to skip her homework, and get her learning from the trials and errors of life.

* * *

"Margot," A.E. says, "Paul Mantz will shoot me if I miss another lesson. I already skipped the last three."

Margot has rarely heard her employer's voice like this: irritated, a touch angry. She is anxious to improve the situation.

"I can give you two hours next Tuesday, from nine to eleven in the morning, but you'll have to cut short your breakfast with the manager of the Bureau of Air Commerce."

"Next Tuesday—that's ten days away."

"Yes, Miss Earhart, but unless you have a duplicate, you're unavailable until then. You're booked solid for the rest of the week. Come see for yourself."

A.E. peers over Margot's shoulder at the calendar. It's full of so many tiny, crowded entries as to give a miniaturist a headache.

"Isn't there any way to shorten this list?"

Margot chews on the end of her pencil.

"Your husband has over six thousand covers over there." The secretary points to some boxes at the other side of the room. A.E. nods. She knows about these. The covers are souvenir envelopes: another of G.P.'s make-cash-quick schemes. Amelia will have the envelopes stamped at major destinations around the world during her trip. When she returns, Gimbels Department Store will shill them: five dollars for an auto-graphed envelope, two dollars and fifty cents for a plain one.

"You're supposed to sign three thousand of them before you leave." Margot says matter-of-factly, then lowers her voice. "Autographing—so simple yet so time-consuming. It's secre-tarial work, wouldn't you say?"

A.E. hesitates. It's forgery, is what it is.

"I signed a few thousand before the crack-up in Honolulu and it *was* tedious."

"If you signed them before, why do you have this lot?"

"Most of the originals were damaged in the crash, I'm afraid."

There was a pregnant pause.

"Please don't think me out of line," Margot says finally, "but I could sign them on your behalf. If I had just a little practice, I could take the whole task off your schedule. It would free up a lot of time."

"I can see that you and I are going to get on, Margot."

Perhaps out of guilt, A.E. does sign a few herself, and has one mailed to Ceci DeRisio. Another disappears into a deep pleat in Margot's skirt. A third goes missing too, though no one knows, until years later. A man named Elmer Dimity, a para-chute expert who is friendly with the aviatrix, manages to get his hands on one of the envelopes from the first batch A.E. signed. He thinks he can use it as a joke. When the aviatrix returns, he'll give the envelope back to her, and she'll gasp in surprise. He'll tell her, against all odds, the mail arrived before she did, and she'll laugh at his cleverness, her grey eyes shining.

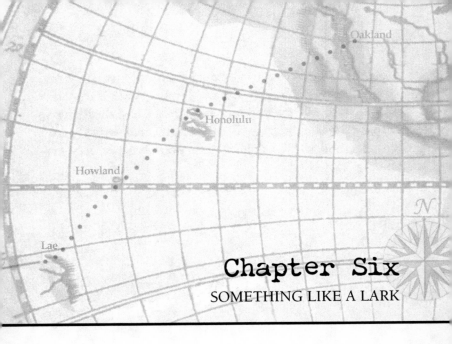

Chapter Six

SOMETHING LIKE A LARK

SHE'S WONDERED IF SHE'LL FEEL A SENSE OF DÉJÀ VU, starting again, but she doesn't.

In the airport in Miami, where Amelia and Fred Noonan will start their second round-the-world bid, she feels instead cold and inert. G.P. drives with her, Fred with his wife, and in a third automobile David accompanies a girl he's met in college—a girl he proclaims, privately, to want to marry. Neither Amelia nor G.P. know whether to take him seriously. At the moment, both have other things on their minds.

She and G.P. leave the hotel at 3:15 in the morning, having been up since 2:00. She still does not feel quite awake, but knows she will have to be sharp and focused for take-off. The mechanics are doing a last inspection now. G.P. hovers behind them, hands knotted. A.E. can see in the distance cars approaching, their headlights flashing along the roads that convene at Pan-American Field. As the minutes tick by, the cars multiply. The occasional flicker turns into a continual faithful brightness. To A.E., the individual lights seem to connect, to form lines: an intricate constellation that culminates with her. An hour after her arrival, there are dozens of vehicles on the outskirts of the airfield. G.P. summons the police to keep order. To build climax.

The number of spectators—five hundred at last count, according to the police—is unexpected. The day before G.P. had predicted the turnout would be low. The papers have allotted page space to other news: Mussolini continuing to shock in Europe, Japan taking a larger slice of world power, and stateside, the violent steel workers' strike in Chicago and President Roosevelt's appointing of another Supreme Court justice. For this new stunt, A.E. doesn't appear before page ten in any major paper.

But five hundred people is still a lot of people, enough to wake a woman up. Enough to make her check herself in a mirror and to rub away her sleep seeds. Her eyes are serious, less wistful than years ago. There are still five hundred people willing to wake in the dead of night for her. She can't take them for granted. This isn't a fluke.

She has an enormous mental check-list to get through before take-off. Her concentration is essential. Fred's wife, however, is determined to speak with her, no matter what. In her stiffly starched shirtdress, she approaches Amelia. She looks like a female Napoleon when she walks: short and swaggering, one hand on her stomach. Not even her three-inch heels slow her down. She stomps straight through mud and puddles of oil, her gaze fixed on the aviatrix's face.

Amelia blinks, waiting to be scolded. Mary's eyes are wild, ringed with a raccoon's mask of mascara.

"Promise me one thing," Mary says upon reaching her.

"What is it?"

"See that Fred drinks his milk, please, every day. He's like an infant. He needs extra nourishment. You should have seen him before we met, poor thing. He was a skeleton, a walking skeleton. His first wife was absolutely neglectful."

Amelia rolls the maps, reports, and coordinates in her hands into a telescope. She is surprised about the milk comment. This is not a subject she would have expected. The spouses of airmen are usually concerned with oxygen deprivation, rowdy layovers, the exaggerated threat posed by exotic foreign women.

At six foot one, wiry but sturdy, Fred is hardly a baby. In sailing as well as aviation, he is world-renowned, a class act, and an innovator to boot. Like anyone intimately entrenched in aeronautics, A.E. knows the trajectory of his career. He quit school early, when he was fifteen. He wanted to be a gypsy. He became a sailor instead, and kept at it for almost twenty years. He loved the seaman's meandering, marauding life. When on land, he stayed in the most unpredictable cities: New York and New Orleans. But he was at sea, mostly, and by all accounts ambitious and heroic, having saved himself and several crewmates during torpedo attacks.

Somewhere along the way he shifted to flying. Pan Am employed him as an aerial navigator. The airline put him in charge of locating and mapping clipper routes across the Pacific. Noonan flew most of these virgin routes himself, testing small, uninhabited islands as stopovers. This is how the world came to know of him—for his pioneering spirit. And this is how G.P. and A.E. came to invite him on her trip.

Why he accepted is another story. A.E. suspects that's why Mary is here, talking in a half-earnest, half-angry voice. She keeps mentioning milk: raw milk, unpasteurized milk, full-fat milk, with cream on top, preferably. A.E. wonders if Mary is obsessed with milk because she is really worried about a different beverage. Alcohol is the tarnish on Fred's otherwise pristine reputation.

"You wouldn't know this to look at him," Mary continues, "but he gets run down very easily. I had to feed him bloody steak twice a day when we first met because the doctor said he didn't have enough iron in his blood. He came to me broken. That woman had some nerve, treating him the way she did."

Mary seems to have a flair for theatrics. A.E., who has been leaning on her bird, stands up straight. In matter of comforting, her height has always been an advantage. The taller she stands, the more authoritarian she becomes. A.E. is used to standing straight and consoling people: her mother, her sister, even G.P. She's used to telling them what to do, and having them listen. She assumes, now, her most confident voice. Mary will remember the tone, if not the words.

"I'll do my best to take good care of him. But you have to remember he's hardly an amateur. Why, the man has rounded Cape Horn seven times! He's the kind of person who sees things through to the end. The kind of person who gets things done."

A.E. stops short of guaranteeing Fred's return. Mary gives her a withering look. Far from appearing soothed, she seems more worried.

"It's an awfully drastic thing you're doing. I admire you for it, but I won't lie: I'm sore that you're taking my husband away less than a month after he put a ring on my finger."

Pretending to consider this statement, A.E. looks over the top of Mary's head. She hopes Fred will appear and take over. The aviatrix is running out of time. The cars are coming. Some of the mechanics are walking away. Then again, if Fred doesn't claim his wife in the next few minutes, G.P. will. He won't let anyone, let alone someone unassociated with the press, have A.E.'s attention too long.

"Mary, Fred's weathered far more difficult circumstances and come back safely, so you have no reason to think this trip will be any different. Besides, as a newlywed, why would he want to stay away?"

When Mary blushes, A.E. feels a surge of relief. Progress.

She realizes she would like to get to know Mary, in other circumstances, in a world where there were more time. She likes her forthright, unapologetic style. The aviatrix watches her move her hand from her stomach to her scalp. Mary scratches at the long cut along her hairline. The wound is dressed with a series of little black stitches, harsh against her fair skin and hair.

"They itch like heck," Mary says.

"That means they're healing."

"That's what Fred keeps saying. I think chicken pox itch. Mosquito bites itch. These are more like torture."

A.E. smiles. She tries not to think about how Mary got those stitches. Two weeks ago Noonan plowed into another vehicle, head-on. He'd been driving in the wrong lane at 40 miles an hour. Miraculously, the persons in the other car, a mother and her baby, weren't injured. The navigator suffered only bruises. Mary fared worst.

From his news cronies, G.P. heard about the accident almost as soon as it happened, and just as quickly tried to convince A.E. to drop Noonan. He was passionate in his opposition. They could get a new navigator, he reasoned.

"The bastard must have been drunk as a skunk."

A.E. agreed, but still would not dismiss Noonan, mainly on account of his loyalty after Honolulu.

Now it's Mary's turn to play down the danger. She picks absently at a stitch. "Oh well, the crash wasn't so bad. And these will heal all right. I don't think they'll be very noticeable. There are a few on my legs that will show worse. But I don't mind, frankly. Gives me another excuse to hide my fat knees!"

"Don't be silly, Mary," A.E. says, perking up. She can see Fred approaching. A second later, he comes up swooping behind his wife, grabbing her about the waist and kissing her on the neck and cheek. Mary laughs mirthfully.

"You ladies are talking about me, I presume."

"Don't you wish!" Mary says. Fred whistles in mock frustration.

Fred looks a good deal older than his fresh-faced wife. Since first meeting him, A.E. has thought him a striking man, a hair's breath away from being handsome because of his elephant ears and extreme thinness. Still, his countenance is pleasing, and he has a pleasant, laid-back demeanor that puts other people at ease, A.E. included.

He nuzzles deep into his wife's neck. Embarrassed, A.E. smiles and turns away. She unrolls the papers again, and read as she walks to G.P., who is chattering with a man holding a camera.

"Need a shot?" G.P. asks. "Look, she's right here. You're in luck. This is your last chance, take it or leave it."

"We've got a stock photo already, sir."

"When you've got the real thing right here? What kind of journalist are you?"

The man looks stricken. As he hurries to take a picture of A.E., G.P.'s arm appears around her swiftly.

A.E. smiles brightly, if falsely, and the flashbulb pops.

"I need to talk to you about the weather reports," she says to G.P., who waves off the reporter. "These are the most current we've got?"

"Yes, ma'am. Freshly picked."

"Okay, well, the winds are lighter than predicted, at least. Did you ask the mechanics about our little science experiment? I think I could have built a better one myself out of a yard stick, a water glass, and some paper clips."

"Which is, essentially, what it's built from, already."

"You're right."

Considering Purdue's eighty thousand dollar donation to her "Flying Laboratory," the equipment G.P. ultimately acquired is a joke. The contraption for catching samples is a four-foot rod with a clamp at the end that holds an aluminum container.

In the air, the container will collect whatever the Electra happens past: bacteria, dust, a bug. A.E. and Fred will collect these samples, describe and date them, and seal them away. Whatever is dredged out of the air will presumably be examined by Purdue's biology department under microscope, upon the Electra's return.

G.P. had written that the "sky trap" is a "state-of-the-art recording apparatus of life at the stratosphere's outermost limit." A.E. can't remember when she heard so much malarkey. The truth is, the sky trap is quick, dirty, and cheap—at best, a yellow-ribbon winner at a grammar school science fair.

"Does Noonan still need to poke it out of the door to the fuselage, holding on for dear life?"

G.P. laughed. "No, let me show you the latest innovative touch. See, now you can attach the rod here." There are a pair of brackets that been bolted to the outside of the ship, where the pole can be fitted.

"These are inaccessible from the fuselage door. They're useless."

"Noonan has long arms. It'll be like he's fishing, only in the air."

She shakes her head vigorously.

"Look, just affix the pole before take-off, all right?" G.P. says.

"You know we can't—we'll be slow and overloaded as it is. We can't add another impediment to our take-off."

G.P. murmurs in his wife's ear. To an outsider, he appears to be whispering "Just take one big sample, eh? On one leg? Then divide the darn thing onto all the slides, and sign them from each day. Purdue's not going to know the difference. To tell you the truth, I don't think their biologists care about this any more than we do."

"Well, you're hardly a champion of scientific authenticity."

"Go ahead and cough into the containers for all I care. You

and Fred are flying experts, not scientists. Let's not pretend otherwise."

She sighs. "I'd feel too guilty. You know, this experiment could be useful, if done properly. No one's ever taken air samples in some of the places we'll be flying over. I can't guarantee we'll catch 'upper-air bacteria,' but you never know . . ."

"Look, if you really want to put in your two cents in the name of science, you can write an article about the range of human reactions to flying when you get back. We'll print it in the Purdue alumni newsletter . . .no, in the *Scientific American*."

"G.P., you're too much."

"I'm being serious!"

"I'd prefer to honor the commitment we've already made to Purdue."

"All right, all right. Look, if the brackets are that bad, you and Noonan can unscrew and reaffix them on one of your stops. It's an easy job, and you have tools onboard. But if we do it now, in Miami, the mechanics are going to squawk like a bunch of hens. They'll need to take turns inspecting every rotation of every screw. They'll find problems and before you know it, we'll need a whole new plane. It'll be 1941 by the time you lift off."

"I see your point."

G.P. ruffles her hair, a pointed attempt at changing the subject. "Well, you look good, kid. Almost rested."

"I'm trying."

"Sure you're ready?"

"They want me to be," she says, nodding at the cars, at the ruck of people.

"The weather's holding for you, like you said. That's a good sign."

With G.P., the world is full of portent and metaphor. She's not sure if he was born this way, or if being bred in a publishing empire made him keen to the power of wording. The power of framing things the right way.

"You know I'll miss you, right?" he asks.

G.P. takes her hands in his and admires them. With hands like this, he thinks, she should have been a pianist: the long tapered fingers, exquisite and refined—completely at odds with her grease-monkey work. As G.P. picks at a bit of grease underneath her thumbnail, A.E. thinks of the far more romantic farewell between Fred and Mary. Sometimes, she and G.P. are more like affectionate siblings than husband and wife.

"I know. But at least you'll keep busy." She pecks him lightly on the cheek, half-waiting for another flashbulb.

It's time. Bo McKneely, the chief mechanic, gives the all-clear signal. Inside the cockpit, A.E. salutes him. The crowd goes berserk. She squints against the airfield lights. Her eyes find David's companion: the girl he claims to love. She is standing very still, her arms straight and rigid at her sides. Her long dark hair frames her face so starkly that she looks like an angel of death. In contrast, the tow-headed David is all life: jumping and waving ecstatically, a skinny-limber cheerleader. A.E. laughs. She's always loved that boy's exuberance. No matter how much he grows, how much he changes in appearance and opinion, a part of him stays perennially childlike. In David, she finds comfort in continuity. In the tumult of life, his joy gives her faith in the stability of small things.

★   ★   ★

Take-off and ascent out of Miami are smooth. After thirty seconds, she knows this won't be a repeat of the Honolulu crack-up, and after thirty minutes, she's feeling calm, nearly serene. She's missed this kind of long foray into the clouds. For the first time in weeks she can concentrate completely on one endeavor. She doesn't have to talk to anyone, check in with Pidge, Amy, G.P., or Mantz. She doesn't have to coordinate, cooperate, collaborate. She is her own captive audience.

She takes pleasure in swooping down low over the Gulf Stream, searching for schools of fish, like swift shadows in the clear water. She thinks she spots a dolphin flinging itself out of the curl of a wave. For a time she listens regularly to the weather forecasts being broadcast out of Miami specifically for her. Then she switches off the knob, and leaves it off. Soon she'll be out of range, but even if this weren't the case, she's tired of listening to human voices.

She has a good feeling about this first leg: the sky is welcoming, the coast is clear. Every once in a while she receives a note from Noonan via their fishing pole. The last one says they've passed an island lighthouse and he's been able to confirm their course and speed. They're right on schedule.

She writes back, "Good, I'm feeling Spartan."

Below, the islands seem to proliferate. Some are populated, with visible outposts, others seemingly void of life. Some are so small as to disappear at high tide. Noonan is familiar with their jigsaw puzzle configuration, having come this way as part of his Pan Am job. He knows the old sea wrecks too, whereas to A.E. each capsized vessel seems freshly brutal.

She'd hoped to make it from Miami to San Juan, Puerto Rico, and then straight to Paramaribo in Dutch Guiana. Fair weather conditions do not hold, however. As soon as she begins flying over South America, she knows that she must land. As the clouds thicken, she follows a muddy river, like an orange snake curling through the startlingly verdant vegetation. Fred directs her to the Caripito Airport in Venezuela. Some accommodating workers push the Electra, tail-first, into one of Standard Oil Company's hangars. Standard Oil has sponsored all of her oil and gas for the journey.

She and Fred climb out, finding their land legs as they walk around the airfield, chatting with curious persons who congratulate them on a nice descent. She brushes away the praise shyly, attributing their success to the beautifully paved runway.

From the sky the town of Caripito is all red roof and terra cotta soil, ringed on the periphery with oil tanks in roughly the formation of Stonehenge. On the ground it's an intimate, sweltering place. Word of her arrival summons more people, both townsfolk and airmen. The humidity seems overwhelming. Everyone is sweating and gesturing, eager to talk with her, to hear if her voice sounds the same as on the radio. Children in cutoff pants run around and play until they exhaust themselves, then seek shade under the hangar roofs, sitting on the dusty ground and sucking on ice cubes and popsicles. Dogs growl, start to fight, then back off and nip at their own tails. Beyond the airfield, clouds gather ominously over the jungled mountains. A few tentative raindrops fall. A downpour, A.E. thinks, would be a relief. She wishes she could peel off her plaid cotton shirt, her long trousers and socks, and let her skin rub flush against the air.

An hour and a half after the landing, the president of Standard Oil Company of Venezuela, Henry Edward Linam, greets her and Fred. He's wearing an ironed white dress shirt, necktie, cufflinks, and shiny black shoes. Considering both temperature and attire, he looks improbably cool and dapper. She thanks him for acting as ambassador.

He smiles magnanimously, gesturing toward the Electra's temporary hanger. A luncheon is being served inside, airfield-style. Her hosts have attempted refinement in rough-and-tumble circumstances: a clean gingham tablecloth on a long plank over two sawhorses, wafts of beefsteak mingling with oil and rust and solvents, a few real chairs interspersed with Pratt & Whitney crates and the Electra's own red-and-white fuel drums. Around the table sit an array of town dignitaries, airfield workers, women, and children. For most of the meal, Linam has Noonan's ear. A.E. listens to them talk about politics in

Central and South America. Noonan's Spanish is passable, as is Linam's English, and the two are soon thick as thieves. Hungry and tired, she's happy to use her mouth to eat.

When the children are finished, they leave the table to play. A few loiter around her, curious, not afraid to touch her. The mothers try to swat them away, but she is happy to have them around. She makes funny faces, plays peek-a-boo with her hands, and frees her pockets of two fireballs, a linty mint, four nickels, three quarters, and a penny. When no one's looking, she gives her glass of grape juice to a little boy who's been eyeing it. He rewards her with a shy, gummy smile, which makes her not care that she's still rather thirsty.

★ ★ ★

She and Fred leave Caripito fresh and early the next morning. The humidity endures, but at least in the sky the wet is tangible: heavy drops pinging off tin. The rain stops after they are in the air an hour.

Fred is used to following the Pan Am route along the coast-line. For a challenge he proposes a different route, sending A.E. inland over uncharted jungle. The thick of trees, in every grada-tion of green, is startling. But for a smattering of lakes and villages, the profusion of vegetation is relentless. Landing would be possible only on treetops.

She sails smoothly, if slowly. Strong headwinds make for pokey progress. A leaky gas gauge adds to her trouble. In Paramaribo, she lands to have the gauge examined. In broken, animated English the mechanic explains two things: the leak is large, and not new. Assuming he is correct and the leak ought to have been detected sooner, A.E. can only conclude that despite G.P.'s best efforts, the quality of the ground teams will differ significantly from stop to stop.

The health of the plane seemingly under control, she turns

her attention to her own body. She's been paying for the nice meal in Caripito. She's made her way through half a dozen cardboard cartons: the receptacle of choice among airsick pilots. Maybe she has food poisoning. The wretched cockpit fumes certainly aren't helping matters. Even on the ground, she's nauseous. Since she and Fred are still in the early stages of their adventure, they agree to pace themselves. If they don't preserve their health, full circumnavigation will be impossible.

They take their time in Paramaribo. By chance, Fred sees an old Pan Am buddy, Carl Doake, in their hotel, The Palace. The men invite her to join them for dinner, which she agrees to. Doake, a former radio operator, has advice to spare on the rest of their jaunt: specifically, which parts of South America to avoid. He warns them against flying over a particularly nasty stretch known for its spiraling winds and staggering air fatalities.

"When you say fatalities, do you mean single digits?" she asks, over a shared plate of soft-turtle eggs and spiny-skinned cucumbers in the hotel restaurant.

"I don't have actual numbers…"

"What is your best estimation?"

Fred laughs at her persistence.

"Let's just say whatever estimation I come up with would be conservative," Doake replies.

Doake departs first, promising to see them off the next day. Fred and A.E. share the rest of the turtle eggs. She watches her partner in the air harpoon an egg with a fork, wondering how her own stomach will react to this strange food. As he chews, she gestures to the raised welt on his head—a scar she's been meaning to inquire about.

"From a torpedo attack. This too," he shows her an ugly keloid at the base of his thumb.

"You survived two of them, I hear."

"Three, actually."

"Impressive."

"Lucky is more like it."

"What did you learn—being that close to death multiple times? What I mean is, if you had to distill the experience into a lesson…" She is honestly curious, if a little nervous. She's asked herself the same question, after near-misses in the air.

"It's luck of the draw: who goes and who stays. I lost some of my best friends in those attacks, and it wasn't for their lack of preparedness or skill. It all depends on where you are on the boat when it's been hit. Nine times out of ten, once you've got a hole in a ship, boy, you're going down."

"And how did you transition from water to sky?"

"I love the ocean. Love it more than the air. Hell, I still travel with a sextant! But I'm getting older, and I want to spend more time doing regular things."

"You want a regular life."

"Well—not quite a regular life," he gestures to the turtle eggs, as if they explain everything. "At sea, you need patience, a lot of patience. You and I are skittish about losing a day of flying here or there. A 48-hour delay seems like an eternity. At sea, that's nothing. When I was younger I sailed on a ship named The Crompton, a great big English beauty. Classic. Square-rigged, tight and reliable as they come. We were supposed to be sailing a few weeks at the most. From Washington State to Ireland over the Pacific, it took us 152 days. Storms, distress calls from other ships, fights, a murder, scurvy—the setbacks kept coming. We ran out of water, food, ale. We ran out of sanity, I'm pretty certain, by the end of it. When you're a sailor, you have to accept that being in a hurry doesn't matter to Mother Nature. Doesn't matter to the waves one bit."

He pauses to drink the last of his whiskey. "What about you?"

She flinches a little. She's not as loose as Noonan, and she hasn't had as much to drink. "What do you want to know?"

"I don't know…anything. Tell me about your family."

"Well, I've got a younger sister, Muriel, and a mother. My father passed away just recently."

Fred nods, offering neither solace nor sentiment. She's glad he doesn't try to fill the silence with half-baked sympathy.

"I feel a bit ashamed to admit this," she goes on, "but part of wanting to fly was wanting to run away, from my mother, in particular. I can't be around her for long without feeling inadequate. She seems to suck away my juices, the good parts of my personality: self-possession, a certain will to achieve. She's a real nervous nelly. When I was a girl I knew nothing would come of me until I'd gotten far away from home and her influence."

"Ain't that natural, though?" Fred says, and it's not a question.

"How do you get on with your mother?"

"She's been dead since I was three. Tuberculosis."

Taking her cue from him, she doesn't fill in the void with an "I'm sorry" or "what a shame," both of which would sound trite.

"I kind of bounced around after she died. My father was still living, but I recall being with cousins and aunts, mostly, and some people I'm not even sure were my kin. One of my uncles, he was close to my mum. He told me a lot of stories about her, and I think she was a little like him: tough-skinned with a big heart."

"I feel terrible, Fred. Here I am criticizing my mother, and you were deprived of yours."

"When I was a kid sometimes I'd see a random woman on the street and imagine she were her—my mother. I'd follow her for blocks. I'd dream she'd take me home with her, take care of me, bake me meat pies, sew up the rips in my clothes, and all the rest.

I'm still a sucker for women. Mary will tell you: I'm like a lamb. I might get tipsy every once in a while. I might duke it out with a fellow in a bar. But I will never, not ever, hurt a female."

An old hurt flickers across his face.

She fishes. "Did your father have a temper?"

Noonan shifts in his chair. She sees how uncomfortable she's made him and tries to withdraw the question. "You don't have to tell me anything."

"You and I are going to be together for weeks, right? It's inevitable; we're going to learn about each other, the good and the bad. We're going to learn everything. I'll tell you the story. I'm sure you've heard worse. And no, it's not about my father. He didn't have a temper, as far as I know, only a perpetually bad memory. Anyway, I was a tyke, seven maybe eight, living with a second cousin on my mother's side. She had no business minding me, this poor lady. She had no money. She couldn't afford rent. And there were so many of us, mostly kids, in her tiny matchbox apartment. She had men who helped her out, gave her money. She called them "her gentlemen friends"—I still remember that! This one guy who was around the most, he was the worst of the lot. One night I went to bed—I used to sleep in the pantry, can you believe it? Below the shelves there was a space about four feet long, and that was a lot where we were living, believe me. Anyhow, I went to sleep, thinking no one's going to bother me in the pantry in the middle of the night. Well, when I woke up, I see this face—a woman's face— but disfigured and bruised-up bad. She's curled up against me close. Her face couldn't have been but an inch from mine. I see two black eyes, dried blood crusted around her mouth. It's takes me a few seconds to recognize it's my cousin.

"First thing I did was check to see she was breathing. She was. I asked her if she was all right and she whispered she just wanted to be alone. I crawled out of there, this skinny kid with someone else's blood in my hair, and I was steaming mad. Small or not, I was going to punch the daylights out of her 'gentleman friend.' But he'd already skipped town by then. I heard he came back, months later, and she acted like nothing happened. She took him back. By then, I was in someone else's house, though, far away in every sense."

"Fred, I don't know what to say. That's an awful story."

"The episode soured me to domestic life for a long time. A long time. But I found Mary, eventually, after being with my first wife. Now Mary's the kind of woman a man can depend on. I knew immediately I could settle down with her."

A.E. flinches again. The aviatrix isn't one for discussing marital matters, particularly when they involve women whose wifely attributes probably exceed her own. She's more comfortable talking shop or bantering. Eager to change the subject, she challenges Fred to a battle of wits. She asks him to name something he's accomplished, something he's enormously proud of, and then she'll have a turn, back and forth, until one of them runs out of things to say.

"When I was navigating for Pan Am, I discovered two islands no one knew existed," Fred offers.

"I was the first woman to pilot an autogyro," she says cheekily.

"Fine. But I rounded Cape Horn seven times."

"Oh, I already knew that one."

"Did you know I can juggle five objects at a time?"

"Extraordinary! But not as extraordinary as the fact that I can touch my elbow to my nose."

"I don't believe you. Let me see." She shows him, giggling.

"I know every constellation in the sky."

"I tried out for the circus."

"I can play the harmonica."

"I can play the piano."

Fred grits his teeth. "I've always liked the piano. A melodious instrument and one that…"

"You're giving up!" she interjects.

He smiles ruefully. As Amelia is about to declare victory, a waiter happens by. Fred's eyes light up at the distraction. He snaps his fingers and speaks in rapid Spanish.

"What did you tell him?" she asks.

"I told him to bring back the menu. I'm still hungry. You?"

"No, not really."

"But you have a little room, don't you? For dessert?"

"I do have a sweet tooth," she admits.

"Good, because I already told him to hurry up and bring a bowl of ice cream for the lady."

She is pleased, despite still being a little queasy, and is happy that Fred has decided to prolong the evening. She listens rather languorously as he explains how the name "Electra" comes from a particular star, one of six visible in the cluster Pleiades, of the constellation Taurus.

She tells him she always thought her plane was named after the powerful daughter of Agamemnon and Clytemnestra in Greek mythology.

Noonan takes a moment to consider this, and then replies, "Who's to say? Maybe you're right."

* * *

After almost a week of long flights over Central and South America, aerial life feels as natural to her as walking. Fred tells her she must have been a bird in a past life.

"Which kind?"

"Hmmm…something fanciful but determined, seemingly carefree, but not at all. A songbird. Something like a lark."

In the sky, her mind runs wild. It loves to scamper, and flying gives her the best opportunity to reflect. Mentally she pens the stories she has promised to G.P. for the *Tribune*. On stops she transforms what is in her head onto paper.

Days pass and they are approaching the African coastline, which is covered by a thick fog. It obscures the borderline between water and land. Fred sends a note. He estimates seventy-nine miles to Dakar.

"Turn to 36 degrees."

Yet she's sure they are south of Dakar. She can't put her finger on why, exactly, without physical proof she believes this, but she does, and strongly enough to defy Fred. When the fog thins long enough for her to know they have indeed hit the coast, she flies north. That they are in dry African climes is obvious by the colors beneath her, visible here and there through dusty clouds: drab neutrals, with little vegetation.

Fred sends a note, "What put us north?"

She doesn't respond. As the minutes tick past, slowly, grimly, she realizes Fred was right. They should have veered south upon hitting the coast.

Hours later she sights a small airfield, finally, and sets down. Turns out they are in Saint-Louis, Senegal. When they've grounded and are on foot, Fred tells her, had she listened to him, they would have made it in only a half hour to their chosen destination, instead of wasting so much time reaching a place they never intended to be. He speaks matter-of-factly, not masking his annoyance. She's stepped on his pride.

Briefly they part, so she can rest, she tells Fred. But really her stomach is bad again and she has to relieve herself. She's dreading the prospect. Airfield toilets are notoriously foul, and the one here is possibly the worst she's ever encountered. It's nothing but a hole shoveled out of the ground and enclosed on three sides with collapsed piles of stones, which were once possibly low walls. She squats awkwardly, for fear of her buttocks coming into contact with the stinky, putrid green feces around the hole or the insects that are feasting on it, for fear, too, that someone will come to spy on her, or god forbid, take her picture.

If the amenities in Saint-Louis are rugged, at least communication is modern. G.P. manages to cable her an entire transcription of Eleanor Roosevelt's popular column "My Day," in which she mentions the aviatrix. A.E. smiles automatically when she thinks of Eleanor, and of others: her pal Jackie Cochran, whose sense of humor is ribald and perverse and quite the opposite of Amelia's; and Margot, whom the aviatrix hopes to keep employed for a long time.

Despite having been offended, Fred agrees to sightsee with her later in the day. It's normal for her to look up at the sky, but in Saint-Louis A.E. does the opposite, looking down much of the time. The feet here are uniformly uncovered, with the exception of a couple of pairs of ancient, ill-fitting shoes that were popular in America twenty years ago. She wonders how the women walk so erectly, with so dignified a gait, when the hot soil and prickly growth must continually punish the bottoms of their feet.

She sticks close to Fred. They observe the simple, sturdy huts made of the same earth that surrounds them. She admires the festive-looking garb of the women, their giant brilliantly colored headscarves, and their jewelry, bold necklaces and chunky bracelets that clink against one another busily.

Fred cheers considerably when they stop at a peanut vendor and buy several sacks of salted nuts. The taste of a familiar food gets him smiling and talking. He tells her that nuts always remind him of baseball games and long summer nights. He says that though they must fly 163 miles back to Dakar the next morning, the detour isn't so bad. Maybe it was fated to be thus, for a local mechanic shrewdly points out a crack in the plane's shaft and sets about repairing it.

The next day they arrive, without incident, in Dakar. This is the first time she's been asked to show her passport, so much for all of G.P.'s admonishments about strict local ordinances and rigid officials. She's pleased with the quality of the airport and by the city itself, located on a divine outcrop of land that, from every point, offers arguably the best possible view of the Atlantic.

In the mansion of their host, Monsieur Marcel de Coppet, Governor General, she and Fred are treated to a delicious meal of delicate saffron rice served with a flaky ruby fish she's never heard of. Afterward, the Monsieur insists they attend a reception in celebration of their arrival. It's thrown by a local group called the Aero Club, consisting of pilots and politicians and their well-groomed, coiffed wives. On the bosoms of the latter, she's never seen so many diamonds and sapphires. Amid the bright flashes of gemstones, A.E. loses herself in South African high society ex-pats. She loves the extremes of her existence: swanky parties and bejeweled pageantry one night, bed bugs, bad food, and bare cots the next. Every week a new continent. There's no way to grow tired of such a life.

She floats from person to person, speaking amiably, listening to all, especially to what her fellow aviators have to say about flying through parched Africa. She is warned, alternately, of dehydration, and sandstorms, and sunburns requiring hospitalization. Be sure to carry lots of extra water, a half dozen people tell her. She finds it hard to take them seriously in this opulent, carefree setting, where champagne flutes tinkle.

Having made a couple of lifeless attempts at conversation, Noonan's now a fixture near the bar. She's noticed that he doesn't favor this kind of expensive company. He prefers sailors, gypsies, grifters, and drifters. Shadier characters. Every time she looks at him, he's taking another sip of his whiskey. So much drinking and yet his glass is always full. She wonders how many refills he's had, taking it upon herself to saunter over and ask. She feels light and vivacious, her head spinning from champagne toasts in her honor, and the fresh memory of higher altitudes.

He pats the seat beside his, a chubby club chair upholstered in the exotically speckled hide of some poor creature.

"We'll be off tomorrow, weather permitting," she says. Her voice sounds soft despite her determination to be tough. "It's going to be a rough haul."

"So you're here to warn me. I wondered when you'd remember me."

She's not sure if he's flirting.

"This is a party in our honor—I'm just making the rounds." She thinks of adding, "like you should be doing," but doesn't. A moment later, a tuxedoed waiter walks by and Noonan signals him for a refill. She frowns.

"You've got to slow down."

"Funny, I was going to tell you the same thing."

"Me? Why?"

"You know why."

"Truly, I have no idea."

He chuckles. "You're living life like it's going out of style."

She rolls her eyes.

"It's the truth," he tells her. "You've got no sense of moderation. Someone's given you a nice tall glass of lemonade and you've been sucking it up like it's bottomless. I'll tell you what: you're nearing the bottom faster than you think."

She sips her champagne insouciantly. "I don't care for precious metaphors."

"Precious," he rolls the word over his tongue. "Yeah, right."

"You're the one who's living too fast." She nods toward the drink in his hand. "We've got all of the African continent tomorrow. Why do you think I came over here?"

"Because you like my company."

"Guess again."

"It's understandable—the way you tag after me, like a lovesick schoolgirl. Happens all the time."

She can't help but laugh. He really is impossible. About the matter of his appearance, though, he's right. Bathed and shaved, with his dark hair smoothed back from his forehead, and his infectious, insubordinately applied smile, he cuts a dashing figure.

Their host appears, wanting to introduce the both of them to the rest of the besotted guests. Fred demurs in surprisingly good French. Amelia acquiesces with a "merci beaucoup." That and French for "where is the lavatory?" are about all she remembers from school. She'd rather have stayed and pursued her ridiculous conversation with Fred, but she can never be sure if he likes her company. She fears he's tired of her, being cooped up day in and day out in the same tin can.

* * *

She soaks in bath salts that night, with three fans running in the deluxe sweep of her private bathroom, high-ceilinged and adorned with African flourishes: giant woven baskets and a deep sink, molded from local clay and glazed to a shine. The bath sits adjacent to her bedroom. To A.E. it's as large as a football field, in comparison to the Electra's interior, at least. The next morning she's refreshed, relaxed, just a touch hung over, at any rate ready for the adventure at hand. Having been warned of barometric lows indicating possible tornadoes, she adjusts her course northerly. Stocked with extra water, the Electra passes over the River Senegal and an upper portion of the Niger River. It arrives, almost eight hours later, in Gao, in the French Sudan.

The stopover in Gao is a completely different experience than in Dakar. For one thing, she and Fred don't leave the confines of the hangar. There are no festivities in their honor to attend, and even if there were, she might just have skipped them. She's drained. The brutal African sun has taken a toll. She drank every last bit of water onboard, another gallon upon landing, and is still thirsty. This parched land, she concludes, was designed for camels and dung beetles and not much else. At least her plane gets its fill. The appointed fuel barrels and oil drums are ready and waiting, as is a telegram from G.P. asking her to turn in another three pages about the trip.

She asks the local ground crew if she can get her hands on a typewriter. No one seems to know what she's talking about, and in the end she writes the requisite pages by hand. This is a painful process. Her fingers are still sore from the continuous vibration coming from the controls. She's hurting and resentful by the time she's done. Resentful toward G.P. for not knowing how much she's going through, and for adding to her labor. Resentful, too, that the business of writing has eaten up the little time on the ground that she has, and now she cannot manage a lick of sightseeing, though she had wanted to visit a mysterious-looking pyramid whose photo she'd once seen in a travel magazine.

She paces in and out of the hangar. Every time she looks at the sky, it's completely different, an evolving, kaleidoscopic feast for the eyes. By contrast, the landscape is lackluster. When she and Fred take off, she sees, below, enormous swaths of desert, few landmarks, almost no greenery, and only the occasional camel trail or thin jagged seam of mountain to separate one drab, barren stretch from another. She spots no villages. What she does spot, endlessly, is dust. The painfully dry air lends itself to the stuff. Though she wipes the inside windows incessantly, at any given moment she can run her index finger across the glass and come up dirty.

Over one particularly tedious tract, she writes her name in the dust, in reverse. Mirror-writing, she thinks it's called. She remembers reading about Leonardo da Vinci writing his personal notes this way. Passing over a military base in Niamey, she considers touching down and taking a nap. Fred is in favor. She waffles for a few minutes as they approach, then decides to keep going.

She feels fortunate that they've so far managed to dodge Africa's sandstorms and other legendary hazards. The flat earth obliges landings. With Fred's help she stays on track navigationally, though several times he has mentioned how useless the maps are. He writes in a characteristically frank note that it's as if the cartographers were smoking opium while doing their work.

About halfway across the continent the Electra flies over the gravy brown waters of Lake Chad. It would be easy to mistake this body of water for an ocean, considering its large girth and lack of visible shoreline. She sends a note telling Fred to get them over as fast as possible. She's scared of crocodiles.

"I've wrestled with them plenty of times. You're in good hands." he writes back.

She takes a chance, as she's wont to do, and flies low. No reptiles leap out of the water, snapping their jaws, but she does see plenty of birds: cranes, herons, and long-legged storks. Fred yells something about a hippopotamus. Unfortunately, she hears "hypothalamus," has a flashback of her short-lived medical school training, and passes the animal by the time she realizes what Fred was talking about.

They pause in Khartoum, the capital of Anglo Egyptian Sudan, for two hours merely, to refuel and stretch their legs. After Lake Chad and measureless desert, Khartoum, this small city set next to the Nile, offers something of a relief. She finds herself a quiet corner in the hangar, curls on the floor on a dingy mat, and sleeps for forty-five minutes. Even in the shade, it's brutally hot: a three-digit number. She imagines life must halt daily midday; it's impossible to be anything but sluggish under such a sun.

She's still tired after her nap, and could sleep another few hours easily. Determination triumphs over fatigue, however, and they reboard. The Electra passes closely to Asmara, Eritrea's capital. En route, the landscape shifts profoundly. Flat, forlorn hinterlands transform into bumpy foothills, and further, into vernal, emerald mountains. Meanwhile, warm air from lower ground escalates, skirting helix-like to the top of the mountain peaks, gaining speed as it summits. The winds toss the plane as A.E. attempts to weave around the rocky crooks. Struggling, she thinks, at least the world is in color again.

⋆　⋆　⋆

Clearing the winds, finally, the Electra sounding no worse for wear, she flies toward a clear view of the Red Sea. Along the coasts are shimmering dunes of white. She believes the sand here must be immaculate, cleansed of color by the crashing waves. When she lands in Massawa, however, she learns that the dunes are actually enormous bluffs of salt. Every day the seaport's scorching temperature evaporates untold amounts of water. Natives collect their white harvest with evaporating pans and pile it into pristine crystalline hills, visible from the air.

Her hosts in Massawa feed her well. Seeing all this salt must have given her a taste for it, for she cannot stop sprinkling her fish and vegetables, and indeed, keeps pinching more from the tiny bowl beside her plate. She's always assumed salt to be salt, but Massawa's crop is different. It's potent, full of saporous memory, distinct from the bland, tired stuff that travels to the American dinner table.

After supper an officer shows her and Fred their lodgings. He speaks some English, peppered with a good deal of Italian, what A.E. thinks is Massawa's official language. He takes them to a room that's as fair and clean as the salt piles. It's appointed with fans, embroidered linens, and a particular thrill: electric lights. When he wishes them goodnight, A.E. objects, trying to explain the need for two rooms. The officer smiles at her politely.

"We are not a couple," she says. "We are traveling separately."

"But you and Mr. Noonan arrived together, no?"

Fred smiles mischievously. He's silent as a stone, letting the presumption flourish.

"Yes. Well, not exactly…."

Her face is red. The officer is visibly confused. His eyes scan her bare hand, looking for a ring.

"Oh, you are not married!" he declares.

"Yes, I am married. We are married—just not to each other."

The officer looks to Fred to see what he has done to cause this bout of marital strife. Still quiet, Fred shrugs. The officer leaves, comes back looking even more bewildered, and leaves again. Upon his next return, he's accompanied by high-ranking members of the Italian Army. They talk seriously among themselves, which makes A.E. blush harder. At length, the young officer extends two brass keys.

"Two rooms. They are side by side…together," he manages.

A.E. wishes she knew how to explain this misunderstanding once and for all. She's too tired to be articulate, or to be mortified, but she'd rather not leave this mix-up in their wake. When the officer departs, however, the confusion is still intact. A.E. and Fred loiter for a minute in front of the door to one of the rooms. She stares at the key in her fidgeting hands. Fred stares at her. She thinks of a hundred ways to scold him, but doesn't say anything.

Before leaving her, he says in perfect Italian: "Buonanotte, bella. Sogni d'oro."

★   ★   ★

Communication around the world and back to America can take an entire day. Sometimes by the time the information has been relayed, like a message passed between children in the "telephone game," it bears little resemblance to its original state. When A.E. and Fred depart from Massawa, G.P. assumes they are taking off for Karachi. In fact, they stop first in Assab, on the west Coast of the Red Sea. Hearing nothing about her Karachi arrival from his contacts, G.P. is convinced she's gone down. For the better part of twenty-four hours, he's a wreck. When he hears, finally, that she's alive, and well, he tells her to come back now, immediately. Forget the rest of your trip, he insists.

By wire, she tells him to stop joking.

She and Fred depart from Assab with extra fuel, which they store onboard. The excess fuel at this destination might mean less at another, a result of botched coordination. In any event, she doesn't want to take a chance. It's a two thousand mile flight from the Red Sea to India. She counts each passing mile as a minor milestone. Sometimes the wind pushes her inland, off-course, but she pushes back.

However undesirable the prospect of an emergency landing in Arabia, she and Fred are prepared, reasonably. They have brought special things: long-sleeved shirts; good, solid walking shoes; extra canteens and compasses. In New York she had a letter drafted. It certifies, in Arabic, who she is and what her intentions are—which is to say, she is merely a pilot who has wandered off-course. The translator said he hoped she wouldn't need it, that Arabia wasn't particularly fond of foreigners, especially women.

Over the long flight, thirteen hours plus, her mind wanders frequently. In one daydream, she and Fred crash in the middle of the desert. A hundred furious, turbaned men in flowing white charge toward them on camels and horses, swords brandished. She and Fred decide to douse the Electra with the extra fuel barrels, thus ending their adventure in fiery glory. Though the scene is melodramatic, unlikely at best, she is relieved when the Electra carries them faithfully to their next stop. Touching down in Karachi, she is informed that she has set a record: the first person to make a flight from the Red Sea to India, nonstop. The ground crew claps at her effort. Their respect does not prevent them from spraying her with a nasty-smelling fumigation agent, however. Apparently, she and Fred have traveled through parts stricken with the disease Yellow Jack.

There is talk of quarantine. Fortunately, she and Noonan are let off with bitter glasses of quinine water, only. A pilot and his aviatrix-wife whom A.E. met years ago come and whisk them away. G.P. reaches her a while later by phone. Until she hears his voice, crackling from travel over thousands of miles of landline and short-wave radio, she doesn't realize quite how much she's missed him. Before she knows it, she's crying. G.P. hesitates a few moments, then tells her he's recording the conversation for the press. She stops mid-sob, composing herself even as anger, compliance, and disappointment fill her. This sort of thing is part of their deal, part of the scheme she agreed to when she married G.P. Still, she wishes he would protect her privacy more. She wishes he would be more decent.

She says brusquely, "They tell me I'm the first person to cross Arabia, from the Red Sea to Karachi."

"Great—that will get the reporters talking!"

"Won't it, though?"

"How are you otherwise? Soldiering on? Feeling good?"

She ignores these questions and says, "Well, I'll cable tomorrow with an estimate of when we should get to Howland. Good-bye. See you in Oakland."

No "I love you's." Certainly nothing sweet.

"Good night," he responds, his tone going soft. "I'll be in California, waiting."

* * *

Perhaps the imagined men on camels were portentous. In Karachi she meets her very own camel, who isn't thrilled to make her acquaintance. He snorts and spits when Amelia wedges herself awkwardly between his gaudily ornamented humps. His hostility isn't surprising. The plugs in his nose his owner keeps to lead him look very painful.

As for Fred, he declines a ride of his own. He's perfectly content to stand on firm ground and poke fun at her. She gives the navigator several withering looks, then breaks out laughing. It's hard to be irritated with Fred, even when his jokes go south.

After the silly adventure with the camel, her tour of Karachi continues with a trip to the post office. She and Fred take the souvenir envelopes with them. Amelia watches the Indian postal employees—uniformly tall, thin brown men—stamp them inside. The workers struggle to find space on the envelopes, which are already crowded with international postage. The envelopes have been shuttled through many other hands, in many other places, and they're starting to look a little worse for wear. A.E. wonders how many of them will actually make it home, intact. She hopes for the best. G.P. reports that demand is high.

Awaiting her at the same post office is a gigantic box of plane supplies. An English-speaking employee tells her it's been here for two weeks. The box is from Pratt & Whitney, and its origin is Hartford, Connecticut. The parcel contains about a hundred spare parts. Though the Electra is currently flying nicely, she's glad to have the parts and stows them in the event of future malfunctions. After the post office, she and Fred stay close to their ship. In the hangar, the Electra is meticulously inspected. Loose screws are tightened, oils are changed, wheels checked, windows scrubbed, and landing gear wiped clean of debris. When the mechanics inspect the bug-catching device, they speak among themselves quizzically. She doesn't try to explain its purpose. Her already slight devotion to the apparatus is waning. In fact, during the last few days she hasn't used it at all. There is something else that catches the mechanics' attention: the radio transmitter box. One of the men summons her to look at it. She and the man stand on top of the plane ponderously, their bare feet sliding on the hot tin. The mechanic climbs into her cubby, taps the box, then looks at her and touches his forehead. Something about the box excites him, but she doesn't know what it is. She smiles and shakes her head. She calls out to Fred, but he tells her he can't help: he doesn't know a lick of Hindi. Ten minutes of further, frustrating gesticulation get them nowhere. A.E. doesn't understand why the man is making a fuss: the box has been working just fine.

Sitting on one of the red and white fuel barrels, the word "EARHART" emblazoned in capital letters across it, Fred whistles "My Darling Clementine." A.E. has disliked the song ever since she learned it's about a girl's drowning. Still, the sight of Fred is endearing. After a few minutes he climbs off to get his sextant, which he inspects and cleans. He's a person who loses himself wholly to a task: concentrating so hard that any conversation or peripheral activity might as well not exist. Watching him, Amelia is sure that no one else would be as meticulous a navigator. A few times during the trip she's thought of playing a prank on him—putting a mouse in his toolbox, or mixing a diagram of the human anatomy in with his maps—just to rib him a little. But she fears such a caper might truly upset him. He can be playful, but he's dead serious about his work.

From Karachi they're off to Calcutta's Dum Dum airport, a jaunt of 1390 miles. As the Electra ascends, large birds fly near. It's a flock of fifteen or more. Raptors, she guesses, eagles or hawks, with dark plumage and razor-tipped beaks. She's never had much trouble with birds, her plane being the biggest winged creature in the sky. Yet this is a surly gang. Perhaps they think she's staking their hunting grounds. Maybe they sense an intruder. She must have done something to incite their wrath, for they follow fiercely, diving and swooping. Maneuvering to avoid them, she can't gain speed. The fastest birds manage to outpace the Electra. One charges from the front, hurling itself against the window. With the collision comes a vile squawk and cries from both bird and woman. The animal's body sticks to the glass. A.E. can't take her eyes off the smash of bloody feathers. Finally, after what seems like ages, the plane's drag blows the bird away. The carcass is gone, sending a powerful message to the rest of the flock. They stop their attack. As they slow and the plane speeds ahead, she feels sick with guilt. The incident conjures up the memory of the dead cat. Whenever she thinks of that cat, she thinks of Dorothy, and whenever she thinks of Dorothy she thinks of fidelity, and familial love, and how she hasn't really mastered either.

Well, one cannot be good at everything, she rationalizes. She's grateful, at least, that the bird didn't crack the window.

She's not sure if Noonan knows what's happened. He doesn't write her a note. If he doesn't mention the birds, she won't. The whole experience has left her spooked, frankly. Foreboding as much as expeditiousness keeps her from stopping for quite some time, not even to see the Taj Mahal, a wonder she'd previously yearned to visit.

Like Africa, much of the Indian continent is barren and sandy. After untold acres of nothingness, she's relieved to spy railroad tracks. They march in straight procession toward other signs of civilization: gardens and larger agricultural quilt squares. Diving in for a look, she sees shoots tall as corn stalks.

"What's growing here?" she writes to Fred, who responds with one word: "jute."

Farther on, the railroad tracks lead to a hodgepodge of huts and dirt roads, which turn into buildings, factories, mills, and, lo: a bustling harbor. Scores of ships are hitched in haphazard, amiable proximity. The Electra has arrived to the Province of Bengal's teeming capital, Calcutta. It is by far the largest metropolis A.E. has visited on the journey.

She and Fred are given a dramatic welcome by a sudden turn in the weather. As the plane descends, the clouds throw in their path lightning bolts and precipitation too dense and swampy to be called rain. It's not a downpour either, for the moisture seems to travel horizontally, vertically, even diagonally. Anything that isn't a hundred percent sheltered is drenched within seconds.

Landing is a soppy, dangerous affair. As the Electra founders, and vision decreases to zero, A.E. doesn't have the luxury of picking where to touch down on the landing field. She merely alights, as best she can. The wheels churn up mud, several inches deep. As the plane rolls to an ungainly rest, she marvels at how low it has sunk.

Through the remainder of the day, monsoon rains continue on and off. During one lull, she wanders into the city and through the streets. She feels as if she's in a sick, sad dream. All the moving creatures—people, camels, mules, horses, rickshaws, bicycles, even an elephant—appear ill, worn to the nub. The air smells of urine and rotting vegetables. There is no sewer system here, no wells, no detectable measure of controlling the squalor that such numbers produce. People eat, shit, and sleep all in the same place. There are children everywhere, filthy children, who are hauling things on their backs that an adult would have trouble bearing. They scratch scabs and runny sores on their knees and elbows, and stare at her with big, bright eyes as she walks by. The sight of one little girl nearly brings her to tears. She's been hobbled by an illness, perhaps polio, and one side of her body is shriveled. The girl uses her stronger side to drag the slack weight of the other, giving her the air of a very old, stooped-back woman. Stopping her scavenging in a heap of garbage by the side of the street, the girl holds one hand out to Amelia. Amelia feels inside her pockets although she knows they are empty. She purposely left without a thing—a precaution against pickpockets. Now she regrets having not a coin or a piece of licorice or a handkerchief. She's upset because really what she wants to do is pick the girl up and carry her away from this tough, furious place, and tend to her and make her well. And yet the aviatrix knows this won't happen, not because it can't, or shouldn't, but because she won't let it. She is not a nurturer, not in the long run. The aviatrix smiles weakly at the girl, who doesn't smile back, but returns to picking. Amelia knows very little separates her from this bent little creature, a bit of good luck and geographical distance are all. The truth depresses her. The double whammy of so much poverty in so confined a space makes her feel weak and ashamed. In Calcutta the suffering is simply too vast to take in, and so she doesn't let it permeate. It hits her and slides off her skin. It has to, in order for her own life, wildly indulgent in comparison, to go on.

Except for this walk, her glimpses of street life are fleeting. She remains indoors: a guard as much against the weather as the hardships of the people. In Calcutta, when it isn't pouring, it is scorching hot, and when it isn't scorching hot, it's pouring. Sometimes the two conditions collide in the most intense humidity she's felt since Caripito.

Monsoon season, her local host reminds her, runs June through October. For daring to travel now, he calls her intrepid. He could just as easily have said "stupid" or "stubborn." At night, on an itchy jute mat, she tries to find comfort in the constant dribbles and splashes. At least they squelch the scrabbling of cockroaches, lizards, or whatever is climbing the walls of her room. It occurs to her that had she not crashed in Hawaii, she would have avoided this watery plague. The first round-the-world jaunt had corresponded with far calmer global weather conditions. A more cautious person would have waited a year before resuming. A more level-headed person than she.

She thinks sleepily, but I'm not that person. And I don't regret anything. Not *yet*.

Fred is bunking in the room next to hers. She wonders how concerned he is with the monsoons. Perhaps he is already—wisely—asleep. As for Amelia, she lies awake with a cardboard carton next to her mat. Her stomach is still a mess. After two hours of sweaty tossing, she gets up and swallows half of a sleeping pill, dry. Better not to drink the water.

When she returns to the airfield the next day, the Electra is in the state she's feared: belly-deep in oozing muck. A dozen men slog over to it in boots, swinging shovels. They have been summoned to dig out the plane and burrow tracks in front of it for at least twenty yards. The previous night's rain has worsened the already awful condition of the entire airport. Puddles are the size of ponds. The mud is runny as hot fudge. This being June, the monsoons will be rearing their soppy heads for months to come. Waiting a day or a week would be of no use, she decides, and so they will waste no time. Besides, she doesn't want to stay in India. Those birds—they still haunt her. As soon as the men are done, she insists on boarding. Fred mutters and grumbles from the back as the Electra gets stuck again and again during take-off. Finally it rises with outrageous sloth. It brushes the tops of the bushes growing about the far reaches of the airfield. It falters, a single nod to this stomach-turning, heart-stopping city, and pushes on.

★ ★ ★

Chewing on fennel and cardamom seeds, A.E. advances, over the winding tributaries that feed the Ganges, over miles of rice paddies speckled with pagodas, water buffalo, and ant-sized people in big hats. She and Fred touch down in Akyab, Burma, to refuel. Although they are off in no time, the weather has changed. Winds blow more freely. Violent rains pelt the plane, hard enough to make indentations. A.E. turns the craft around, though she's not sure going back will be any better than going forward. She tries to fly at a lower altitude, to weave between the darkest clouds. The storm finds her anyhow.

Every second is a battle. The winds blast the plane back as soon as she makes headway. An hour passes with hardly any progress. Exhausted and frustrated, she struggles in vain to see out the windows. The distortion caused by precipitation has put her in a trance. Fred abandons his station at the back of the plane. Squeezing into the cockpit, he manages with effort to park himself into the copilot's seat. A limp A.E. hardly notices him.

Fred says he is here to offer fresh eyes. She declines his help, asking him to return to where he came from.

He replies, "Please—let me stay. I'm not trying to take over." This convinces her. A good captain must know when to step up, she thinks, and when to step down. Fred offers what she no longer has: effective strategy.

"Fine, you direct," she yells hoarsely over the lashes of wind. She becomes a pair of hands as he guides them back to the airfield in Akyab.

To the exhausted aviatrix, the plane looks relieved to be back in its old hangar, under shelter for at least a little while. She accepts a quaff from Fred's flask. She strokes the Electra. The rains have washed off the paint from the tips of the wings. Before leaving to go to sleep, she promises her plane a fresh coat, as soon as possible.

The monsoons continue to slow them down. Her second attempt out of Akyab is also problematic. She lands, prematurely, in Rangoon. A.E. interprets the stop as a sign that they should cut their losses and sightsee. The American counsel here, surprised and delighted by their arrival, offers to be their guide. As they take a walking tour, the aviatrix listens rather distractedly to his descriptions of Rangoon's architecture and history. She spends so much time cloistered in the Electra's cubby that the everyday bustle of life is increasingly jarring.

She tries to acclimate by studying the people who pass by. She pays special attention to the women, who wear bright, flowing clothes, and keep their faces down. They are deliberately separate from the men, walking in their own groups and traveling in their own streetcar compartments.

Determined, if fatigued, at the beginning of the walk, A.E. deteriorates quickly. It's not surprising that she should feel ill. As her mother used to say, cold and wet are the makers of flu. A.E. hasn't been cold, but she has been wet. Her garments are perpetually damp, even those kept sealed inside the plane in her suitcase. Her nose is clogged with yellow gunk. Her throat is itchy. She isn't hungry, but the waistband of her skirts and trousers are much too loose. Despite all this, she doesn't turn down an opportunity to visit Burma's Shwe Dagon Pagoda, an enormous golden structure that flashed at her from the air like a 24-carat lighthouse. Fred, who looks as sick as she, says he has no interest in going inside.

"Oh, come now. You must. When will you have this chance again?"

"I don't know and I don't care."

Aviatrix, navigator, and guide are all standing outside the pagoda. It seems criminal not to enter, having come this close.

"Why not?"

Fred's acting so peculiar. There is something he isn't telling her. She follows his gaze, to the people entering and exiting, to their ankles and bare feet.

"Why, you don't want to take off your shoes? That's nonsense!"

He shrugs. When she makes another feisty remark, he ignores it. She stops trying to change his mind. She touches her long skirt, self-consciously. It doesn't suit her sensibility or her style. Funny how when she's dressed most femininely, she feels least attractive.

The guide, oblivious to any tension, continues to chatter

away. Fred begins to inch back. Finally, he detaches himself from their group, saying he can't think of anything except sleep.

"Not to worry," says the guide. "I'd be delighted to personally escort you inside, Miss Earhart."

She smiles, trying to hide her irritation. Through the corner of her eye, she watches Fred weave into the crowd. The guide insists on purchasing her a miniature gong, a common souvenir sold in the stalls around the pagoda. It's a ridiculous present to store in the precious real estate of the Electra. She lets him buy it for her anyway. The gesture seems to make the guide feel good, even if it doesn't cheer her very much.

*　*　*

From Rangoon's golden trappings it's on to Bangkok, and then to Singapore. En route, the view turns as lush as it was over South America: a hundred greens splashed artfully on the canvas below. The jungle creeps with determined, tyrannical force over mountain, hill, and valley. Here and there, hardly making an impression in the crowded vegetation are mines and rubber plantations. A.E. imagines the trails and roads leading to them must be chopped anew every day, or lost. She writes to Fred to ready the parachutes just in case. Landing by plane would be impossible. Of course, parachutes have their own perils: she has heard of men caught in trees, stranded, hanging, till death.

Fortunately, her luck holds: she and Noonan make it to their destination without incident. The Singapore airport is perhaps the best they've encountered: world class, a nine-million-dollar dazzler that geographically and aesthetically bridges East to West. She hopes the mechanics are as impressive as the facilities. Leaky, creaky, and slow since Akyab, the Electra is showing signs of true distress. The plane is rolled into a hangar and receives a tune-up immediately. The promptness surprises her. It's the end of the workday: six o'clock p.m. local time. Yet the star-struck mechanics promise they will work into the night, for her. By nine they have conferred with a translator, who explains the plane's ills. They are as numerous as she suspected. For the first time, A.E. delves into the spare parts box she received in India.

Despite setbacks in machinery and weather, she's pleased. She and Fred are making sound progress. They can feel the momentum building, and can practically taste the end of their tour. Fred, who has been unable to shake his cold, is downright gleeful. Before boarding for their next jaunt, Java, he conveys the sum of his anticipation with one droll, toothy smile. She realizes she's the only person to know all the risk and glory behind it.

Gorgeous greens transform into vibrant blues as the Electra leaves Singapore. The plane floats above deep waters, alternately the color of cornflowers, blue lobelia, and grape hyacinths. The weather is clear, visibility excellent. Through turquoise shallows, small islands sprout up cheerfully. Boats shuttle between them, their jaunty white sails flapping. Closer to the islands, the sea pales, turning translucent as it nibbles along the shores, leaving long trails of frothy foam.

Watching all this, Amelia thinks for what must be the millionth time: it's beautiful to fly—endlessly, hauntingly beautiful.

In Bandoeng, West Java, G.P. phones her. She still feels cool toward him and wonders if he is recording their conversation again. Every word is screened and sanitized before leaving her mouth. Truth is, she'd rather be exploring Java's volcanoes then checking in with her husband. Abandoning her mental script, she says just that. There comes a silence. She doesn't know if G.P. is angry or if the interruption is a hiccup in the long, circuitous line.

He laughs, finally. "You don't permit me a moment's peace, even on land."

She thinks he does the same to her, but doesn't say so.

The climb up one of West Java's famous volcanoes—an adventure that requires shoes—appeals to Noonan. He and the aviatrix chat as they huff and puff their way up. She notices that their legs are the same length, their strides nearly identical. Ahead, sniff dogs scamper, their noses raised. The volcano is still active, and the closer to the summit, the worse the stink of sulfur. Crinkling their noses, she and Fred quip about who will be able to run down faster should lava start spewing. Although she's enjoying herself, she feels guilty about not supervising the technicians working on the plane. It's not that the mechanics are inept; on the contrary, they strike her as quite competent. It's just that more and more of the plane's equipment is breaking down. Even the first-class maintenance in Singapore didn't stem the tide.

By sundown the plane is still in bad shape. She resolves to get a decent night's rest even so. She and Fred are staying in the best rooms of a newly built hotel. For the remainder of the journey, they will not have such luxurious accommodations. Bouquets of fresh flowers perfume her room. A maid knocks at her door, balancing a loaded platter of fruits, chocolates, and coffee on one hand. The pilot turns down everything, not wanting to ruin her sleep. Despite the precaution, she has a bad night.

By late morning the next day the Electra seems up to snuff. A.E. and Fred bid Java goodbye. There departure is premature, however. Upon takeoff technical problems persist. The aviatrix turns the vessel around and returns to Bandoeng, where the chief mechanic tells her one of the engines has burned out. Necessary repairs will require days, not hours. Agitated, consumed with impatience, she tries to take her mind off the delay by driving to Batavia, the capital of the Dutch East Indies. Here, she passes up newly caught fish wrapped in banana leaves for the traditional multi-course meal known as rijsttafel.

She gorges herself, though her stomach is still off. Afterward, she takes a long walk alone. She distracts herself from her anxiety by window-shopping. Batavia is full of enticing little shops, where she could easily spend a month's earnings on odds and ends. For several minutes she lingers in front of a metal worker's studio. Inside, she browses through his collection of hand wrought knives. She selects a small weapon with a carved tortoiseshell handle. It's an exceptionally pretty, exceptionally sharp piece. She decides its usefulness at least exceeds the gong's. Affixing the accompanying sheath to her belt, she untucks her shirt and resumes the walk feeling considerably better.

It is June 27, 1937, by the time she and Fred depart again. With a stop in Koepang, they cross the Timor Sea and land in Port Darwin, Australia. A.E. realizes they're back in civilization, with all the fear and cautiousness it cultivates, when they are corralled from the plane into an adjacent medical facility. A doctor ushers her behind a partition and checks for ticks, piranha bites, anaconda squeeze marks, and every other ailment one could imagine. He asks her if she's been drinking boiled water, and she nods. He asks her if she's gotten mosquito bites. She nods again. He proceeds to inspect her head to foot, growing shyer as he inches his way down. Naked, bony, sunburned, and bemused, she does her best to support a conversation about the length of mosquito proboscises. The doctor's face is very red. She wishes the bald patch near her ear weren't there. She's wishes her legs and armpits were shaved, her pubic hair not so wild. She's not unduly embarrassed, however. With a stranger, this sort of intimacy is, at worst, uncomfortable.

* * *

The pearl diver she meets in Port Darwin is skinnier than both she and Fred: a feat. She spots him on a pier, where she and the navigator are parked with a couple of sandwiches, and a long list of technical issues they need to address before making the leg from Lae, New Guinea, to Howland Island. Fred's chronometers are high on the list. They have malfunctioned chronically, as has his gyroscope.

The diver approaches them out of nowhere, fearlessly, not seeming to know, or care, that his arrival halts conversation. A.E. is in the middle of convincing Fred that they won't need the parachutes—what use could they possibly be over the South Pacific? They are no longer lifesavers, just extra weight. It's an argument she will later win.

The diver wears a pair of sun- and salt-faded cut-off dungarees. They hang on his bony hips with the help of a rope belt. His toenails, the first thing Amelia notices about him, are dirty, yellow, and so long they are curled at the tips. He takes a wet satchel off his back and shakes it. Whatever is inside clinks.

"The last catch of the day," he tells them.

"Doesn't sound like fish to me," Fred replies.

"No, sir. Oysters."

Though it's late afternoon, the sky is still bright. A.E. squints to get a better look at the stranger's face. She can't tell how old he is. He's wrinkled, but so are many who make their living on the water. His eyes are what stump her. Set very deep, too deep to search, they give away nothing of his experience. The pupils are milky, as if with cataracts. He's missing half a finger on his left hand. She notices this as he runs the hand over the stubble of his shorn head, explaining that he collects oysters for a living. His accent is thick. She understands what he's saying only after running through the oddly inflected syllables a second time in her head. The man says he can hold his breath underwater for twelve minutes, that he used to take thirty plunges a day, but is down to ten. His body is not as strong as it was, his heart races now. Still, he's known among the divers for having good fortune. Good luck when it comes to pearls. Jangling the sack again, he tells them he plucked these shells from a particularly fertile bed, in particularly deep waters.

A.E. doesn't realize he's a peddler until he asks, outright, if they'd like to see the oysters. She nods. He spills a few of the shells onto the rocks. One or two crack, releasing a nauseating, fermented stench.

"Doesn't smell like you caught these today," Fred says distastefully.

"These ain't for eating."

"You think there's a pearl in this batch?" she asks.

He seizes her in his odd, ambivalent stare. "Reckon there is."

"Do the pearls vary depending on where you find the oysters?"

"Yep. The deeper the water, the darker the pearl. Found black ones just twice, far down. Fainted as I swam up. I floated to the top and made it out alive, hardly. When I woke up on the beach, I wasn't sure how I got there."

She's not sure why, but thinks she would believe just about anything this strange man had to say. If her trip around the world were a myth, then he would be the oracle who appears out of nowhere to convey something urgent, something that will forever alter the course of her story. Fred shakes his head reproachfully as she fishes for money in her pocket.

"Is there a black one in this set?" she asks.

"No, ma'am. The chances aren't good. I found black ones just twice, like I said."

She takes out several American dollars, glancing at Fred, who's looking out over the harbor. Dapples of fading sun skip on the waves.

"Tell me," she says, counting the bills cautiously, "why do you sell the oysters whole? Why not open them yourself and sell whatever pearls you find?"

"People don't buy my oysters for the pearls, ma'am."

"So why do they buy them?"

"For the chance to find their own pearls."

"You think they buy a chance at luck?"

"Yes, ma'am. I reckon so."

She's been squinting for so long her eyes feel strained. Even with the lengthy stopover in Java, she's not fully recuperated, physically or mentally. The muscles in her face are taut and hard, the same as when she has to pose for photographs for a long time.

"How do I know these oysters aren't a bunch of duds?"

"I can't say for sure what they are."

She realizes suddenly what it is about the man's eyes that make them so confounding, aside from their murkiness. He hasn't blinked, not once.

"Sir, how do you see your oysters? When you're diving?"

"You don't have to see 'em. You feel for 'em. See, that's how I lost this." He waggles his stumpy finger. "Poked it in someone's hole. It didn't like that!"

His scampish mirthfulness makes her uncomfortable. The conceit that he has a secret wisdom to impart starts to fade. Why, she thinks, he's just an everyday huckster who happened to stumble upon her at leisure and willing to listen. Handing him two dollars, she puts the rest of the bills away with deliberate finality, hoping to send him away.

"Much obliged to you," he says, shaking the remaining the shells into a toppling heap. He takes the dollars so nimbly she doesn't quite register the transaction. After scooting swiftly across the trap rocks of the pier, he scampers onto the beach, and out of view. Fred continues to stare at the water.

"Why in god's name did you buy those?"

"Out of guilt for having a little money, I think."

"You're really going to open them?"

"Yep."

"Have you ever opened an oyster before?"

"Nope."

She pulls the knife from the sheath at her waist and tests the blade with a light stroke of her finger. Still as sharp as when she bought it. Picking up an oyster, she inserts the tip into the blubbery flesh at the seam. With effort, she cuts partway around the shell and tries to pry the two halves apart. They don't budge. With a sigh, Fred gives her his full attention, finally, reaching for both knife and oyster.

"Gimme those, you're going to hurt yourself."

"No I'm not."

"Just let me do it, will ya?"

She relents. Holding the oyster level, he reinserts the knife at one corner of the shell, paring swiftly and adroitly. He pulls open the upper shell like it's a top on a hinged box. With a quick jab, he clips the last bit of clinging muscle. She memorizes his technique, thinking that his store of arcane abilities is endless.

Tipping out the briny juices, Fred looks into the flesh on one side of the shell, the opalescent sheen on the other.

"Voila," she says.

"'Voila?' No pearl."

She gestures to the spilt oysters all around them. "No matter. We've got plenty more chances."

"You really are a gambler, you know that?" In silence, he opens a few more. She wishes she had another knife.

"Have you ever just sat next to the water and done absolutely nothing?" he asks, starting to make a pile of the discarded shells. Busily, she arranges the unopened oysters into a second pile.

"Nope."

"Why do you always have to be doing something?"

"I don't know. That's the cloth I'm cut from, I guess."

"Made to be busy."

"Made to be *useful*."

"Your definition of useful's different from mine."

"Why do *you* always have to be difficult?"

He wipes the knife onto his pants' leg. "A few more days and we'll be through," he says.

She shrugs.

"What? Are you sorry?"

"I don't know. There's so much we haven't seen. We had some time in Java, but not very much, and none at all in other places, no time to stop and take a breath and take it all in. For three weeks now I've been telling myself 'next time, you'll see that next time,' but in all honesty, who knows when that will come. Maybe never."

"You know what I think? I think if you had to make this trip again, you'd do it exactly the same. It boils down to the fact that, at any given moment, you'd rather be flying than on the ground."

"Oh, that's not true. Well, maybe you've got something."

"Maybe? If there's one thing that's perfectly clear, it's that you live, eat, and breathe the sky, Amelia."

There could hardly be a less romantic moment, considering the stink around them, the spoilt shellfish and screeching seabirds that have taken a keen interest in the sudden trove of food. Even so, she thinks she would like to lean over and kiss him.

"When we're done," she says cautiously, "not immediately, but maybe months, maybe a year from now, do you think we'll fly again, together?"

"Don't see why not."

There is something else she's wanted to say for some time now, and she does: "Because, after all this, I think, no, I'm sure, that you know me better than most."

"Likewise."

She looks at him searchingly. As usual, she can't figure out if he's indulging her, if he's sincere, if her admission means an ounce of anything important. The heaps of shells lay between them: forty or fifty in the discard pile, and the oysters that are still whole. A surprise fumble sends the knife into Fred's palm. It's a doozy of a cut. She makes him get up and dunk his hand in the salt water to clean it. There's some gauze in the plane's first aid box, but the plane's in a hangar, a good mile's walk from here.

She gestures toward the oysters. "Forget the rest. You were right—I was duped."

Ignoring her protestations, he keeps going. She avoids looking at his hand, at the blood that is trickling down his arm as he flicks the knife. She's too busy feeling foolish and blame-worthy; she doesn't see the moment of revelation: the splitting of one oyster, quite like the rest of the oysters, exceptional in no way, except for the gleaming pearl inside.

He whistles in surprise and plucks it out carefully. It's globular, asymmetrical, nearly the size of a dime. "Well, it's not black."

"But it's lovely all the same."

He rinses it off in a tidal pool and rubs it clean and dry with his shirtsleeve. Then he hands it to her.

"Are you sure?" She thinks that maybe he would prefer to give it to his wife, but doesn't want to say this aloud, for fear that she will sound out of line.

"For the Howland leg—good luck," he insists.

They leave the remainder of the shells; the birds will have a heyday. It's getting late. They need a status report from the mechanics. As they walk to the hangar, the moon heralds a darker, colder sky. Her pants are wet from sea splash and damp stone, the backs of her legs still indented with the impression of craggy rock and barnacles. She's chilled, shivering, but happy, happy and lightheaded, like a kid on Christmas Eve. When they reach the plane, she finds the first aid box and helps Fred swaddle his hand with gauze. The result is silly, an outrageously oversized mitt. He dodges and weaves playfully, a one-gloved boxer.

She thanks him again as they part ways. He wants to make sure all his equipment is in order. As for A.E., she's got work to do, too. She's intent on writing a few more pages for G.P., a few words about the flora and fauna of the air, which she is now completely neglecting to collect for Purdue. She tries to gather her thoughts, but she's too giddy to sit still, let alone write. It's the pearl that's got her excited. She decides to get up and package the parachutes and other discarded things. She writes down her address in Rye and pays the hotel concierge to send the items by ship. When she's through, the concierge reaches to take the parcels from her, but she hesitates. He concierge smiles encouragingly. He's ready to do whatever she wants. A.E. recognizes his accommodating expression. And he recognizes her face, her name.

"Will you send this too, please?"

She unclips her beloved silver flying wings from her blouse. "It should be sent to a different residence. Here…"

She copies the address from the letter she carries in her pocket, the letter she has consistently transferred to whatever outfit she is wearing, one to the next, ever since Hawaii. The wings will go to the young fan her secretary told her about: Ceci DeRisio. A.E. is not exactly sure why she is sending the wings, right now and not before. She hadn't even considered the prospect until this moment. Perhaps in receiving the pearl from Fred she feels she should bestow a gift of her own. A favor given for a favor received. The concierge nods courteously, and in her own private universe, balance is restored.

* * *

Since Java she has assumed accommodations will be rough—floor mats or bare ground; no toilets, hot water, or electricity. Mentally, she has prepared for camp-like conditions, and so is surprised when their lodgings in Lae turn out to be clean and modern. She and Fred take the last two of the dozen rooms available in a commodious one-story lodging house.

"Who are your other guests—Americans like us?" she asks the manager, to make conversation.

He doesn't answer at first. She wonders if he speaks English. After a lull, he replies with a sniff: "They are all, miss, Europeans."

She and Fred rest for a bit, then borrow an open-top jalopy from the lodge and take a bumpy ride around the coast. On the way they see some of these so-called Europeans. Their particular clothes and wrinkled, parched-looking skin separate them from the natives, as do their vehicles: heavy trucks loaded down with industrial mining equipment. Visitors do not come to Lae to be idle. They seek gold, which lurks in abundance in the hills. The plunder of precious metal is on display in new seaside homes of palatial proportion. The manses cling tightly to the slim tracts of earth between shore and jungle, as if in fear of nature's power from both directions.

A.E. and Fred drive and drive. Feeling rebellious, they nearly bust their car's tires careening beyond road and trail. They veer through knee-high grasses, past scarlet hibiscus, jubilant trumpet flowers, and orchids growing in brilliant profusion. Iguanas skitter by, yellow-eyed and alert, some leaping with abandon in the overhead eucalyptus trees. Under the blazing sun A.E. and Fred forget that Lae receives nearly as much rain as Calcutta. Their tires are soon stuck in mud, spinning spastically. She takes over at the wheel as Fred gets out to push from behind. The tires revolve in stagnant frustration, ever deeper. They fling mud onto Fred's face and clothes. She stifles a giggle. It takes a rock on the gas peddle and four hands on the back bumper to get out of the rut. She and Fred dash to catch up with their runaway ride, jumping in merrily and swerving in time to avoid colliding with a clump of shrubs.

Finally they find their way back onto a road that winds to a coconut grove: lines and lines of trees swaying like lean, lithe dancers. Farther on, men noisily herd pigs and chickens on swatches of land sawed out of the jungle. Women tend to clinging children.

A.E. is fascinated by the appearance of the natives. They seem to wear the natural world repurposed: feathers and skins and furs as clothes, yellow and red ochre paste dabbed on the skin. Their satchels and belts are woven from reeds, and their jewelry is of cowrie, bone, clay beads, and nut shells. The people of Lae seem to represent the boundary between wild and civilized cultures, and Lae itself: the boundary between order and disorder, safety and strangeness.

It's dinnertime when she and Fred make it back to the hotel. She's due to meet with a local couple who have settled here from London. Both are former pilots and they have sponsored the Electra's mechanical costs here. G.P. set up the dinner as a kind of reimbursement. She will give the couple an hour or two of her time in return for their generosity. She assumes Noonan will join them—that he will *want* to join them. But he tells her he has his own plans. "It's business," he says when she frowns. He's liaising with a member of New Guinea's Civil Aviation committee, hunting for fresh details on how to approach Howland. She wishes she hadn't confirmed dinner already. If she could have excused herself, she would have joined Fred. Then again, he doesn't invite her.

"You know, these people I'm meeting may have information on Howland, too."

"Well, find out what you can. You can give me a recon report afterwards."

Resigned, she prepares for the dinner, bathing quickly. She's running late, but takes an extra few minutes to shave her legs. Her razor is dull and the resulting red scrapes and bumps are hardly better than the hair. She breaks off a piece of aloe vera that's growing beside the patio adjacent to her room. She squeezes out its jellied insides and rubs it on her calves and thighs. Her skin feels instantly cooled, soothed. She paws through her suitcase in search of her last remaining clean clothes, which aren't really clean, just not visibly dirty. With a sigh she settles on a blue cotton blouse, less rumpled than its sisters, and a long khaki skirt. No trousers in Lae; she already sticks out like a sore thumb. The waist of her skirt is much too loose. She cinches it with a belt, but that, too, is loose. After two seconds' consideration, she takes it off and makes an extra notch with her knife. In the mirror that hangs over the wash-basin, she watches herself dab attar of roses, bought on a whim in India, behind her ears. She fluffs her hair. Not altogether satisfied with her appearance—lately she seems every bit her age—she sets off.

After exactly one hour with the couple, the aviatrix has had enough. They are nice company, civil company, almost painfully polite with their stiff British manners, and yet Amelia can't remember a word of what they said. Lately, when she's not flying, she's always distracted. She keeps her head down on the walk back to the hotel. Her ears are perked. It's dark now, and she's not sure if it's safe for females to walk alone. Better to be vigilant. At the plaintive cries of night animals, she hunches her shoulders and picks up her pace.

Entering the lodge, she sees that the manager she and Fred met earlier is still on duty. He's sitting on a chair behind his desk, head tilted, snoozing. He awakens when she strides over to him, although she's light-footed and tentative. She asks if Noonan has come back. Her tone is nonchalant, as if this is a purely minor matter.

She must make sure her crew is well rested, shipshape, she says with a smile.

The manager replies that he hasn't seen Mr. Noonan. She takes a chance and knocks on Fred's door, but he's not in.

Returning to the manager, she asks: "Where do men normally go around here—to relax?" Her voice has gone up an octave. She wonders if he believes her façade of casual curiosity.

There is a bar separate from the hotel's restaurant, he says, in a somewhat annoyed tone that suggests it's separate for a reason. Undeterred, she ventures there. What it is, really, is a shed—thrown together without much care or money or, it seems, architectural reasoning. It's located in back of the hotel, in its proverbial shadow, uncomfortably close to the jungle's hungry edge. From the outside it would seem a low-ceilinged place, but to enter she has to walk down several steps. The shed is half-underground physically, atmospherically too. It is indeed, as the manager insinuated, a hideout.

On the door hangs a weathered sign reading "Ricky's." She thinks of the word "underbelly" when she opens the door, actually says it aloud. She squints at the knockabout tables, the smattering of stools and chairs. Somewhere in the dark, humid air, an invisible radio plays maudlin violins.

She finds Fred and his companion at the bar. The men are loud and jocular, two words she wouldn't normally attribute to Fred. Nevertheless, it's unclear to her if he's drunk, or just happily unwound. He's sucking on a cigar, his long legs sprawled out beyond the stool. His feet are planted on their heels. Fred's companion looks equally relaxed. It's a party. A party of two, and though Noonan's expression is affable, she feels like she's intruding.

"I wonder when you two night owls will be calling it quits?" she asks. She didn't plan to say this. She's surprised when it comes out of her mouth. She is surprised by her tone: persnickety schoolmarm. Truth is, had Fred been alone, had he asked if she wanted a nightcap, she would have said "yes."

"Fred, do us the pleasure of an introduction," the companion says. Unlike Fred, he's unmistakably drunk: bleary-eyed, bleary-voiced.

"Michael Colliope, meet Amelia Earhart: aviatrix extraordinaire. Amelia Earhart, meet Michael Colliope: first-class scamp."

"Come on, darling. Take a seat and indulge us in some female company. I've had enough of listening to your crazy friend. I imagine you have, too."

"Oh, I'm afraid I can't. I'm done for the night."

"Come on, lass. Don't be shy. You're on a different clock now—you're on the other side of the world, New Guinea time."

She winces. Unless she agrees, she'll sound shrill. She's tired of being a killjoy. She tries to decline again, less vigorously. "Thank you—another time, perhaps."

Noonan's wide grin shrivels.

"Oh, all right, why not," she says. "One drink."

She tries to take a seat beside Noonan, but Calliope scoots over, patting the stool between them. He pulls his seat closer to hers. Their knees brush. She crosses her legs primly, toward Noonan, who orders her a scotch, neat. She grits when she tries it. After a few sips, it goes down with less fire. He orders her another, and one for Calliope.

The night unfurls. The barkeep changes the radio station and now the sad violins are gone. A newscaster is talking in German. The barkeep lights a lantern, which he hangs from the raftered ceiling, and a few candles, which he scatters among the tables. Despite the illumination, the night feels grayer than ever. Amelia looks from Noonan to Calliope. Through the cigar smoke their faces are shadowed and distorted. Their proximity makes her nervous. She has trouble concentrating; their features seem oversized, noses and lips magnified. Their voices compete with the foreign tongue on the radio.

She's on her third scotch when the sailors come in. There are four of them, in crisp, smart uniforms. Two females follow in their wake. The girls seem to Amelia in better definition than everyone else, as if glowing internally, like fireflies, in their own phosphoric black light. They have straight, dark, waist-length hair, which they rake with their fingers. Their bodies are child-like, thin-hipped and small-boned, with almost no breasts to speak of. Upon closer study, A.E. sees they are of different ethnicity. They are of different age, too, probably by at least a decade. The younger, who resembles the women A.E. saw in Rangoon, has round doll's eyes, made bigger with sooty powder, a moony face, and wide, flat cheeks. By contrast her companion has close-set almond eyes, a scar under her nose suggestive of a hare-lip not quite corrected, a beauty mark drawn on her cheek, and zealously tweezed eyebrows. Both girls wear long skirts, cut modestly, almost demurely. When they sit, the skirts open at the sides. The skin revealed by these hidden slits, though not unseemly, is provocative. In Lae, women seem to wear clothes to adorn rather than to conceal, and yet, in this clandestine lair, thick and beery with male bravado, even a flash of a woman's skin is like a gleaming silver lure sunk in dark waters.

"The night just got a little longer, eh?" Colliope says, over Amelia. Fred snorts inscrutably.

One of the sailors comes to the bar and orders drinks. He's an English-speaker with an Australian or New Zealand accent. He can't be more than twenty years old, Amelia thinks, looking at his boyish face. As the sailor waits for the barkeep to gather the drinks, Colliope introduces himself. He asks when the fellows came ashore. They've already been here a fortnight, the sailor tells them. They've come by way of the Solomon Islands. They're doing exploratory work for the Seamen's Union of Australia. The girls? He's not sure how long they're here for. Seem to be permanent transplants with a steady income. Shipped over for a reason, if you know what he means. Howland Island, sure he's heard of it. A wee mite of a place, but not impossible to find. Used as a landmark in these parts, never much as a docking point. His comrade Trevor knows more about it, why don't Noonan and Calliope join them for a drink? He looks toward Amelia courteously, if dismissively, as if she were an elderly auntie who forgot to go home. He doesn't recognize her, or he doesn't care to.

A.E. straightens her back, and uncrosses her legs. She drinks her drink.

Calliope accepts the offer. After the barkeep delivers the beers on a tray, the men take turns glancing at her uneasily. She is supposed to beg off now, to yawn and go away quietly.

She turns to Fred, "Did you fix the chronometer?"

When he doesn't respond, she repeats the question. He sips from his glass and she tries to remember when he last ordered for himself. She's almost sure he's nursing the same drink as when she got here.

"Everything's under control."

Back where the sailors are sitting, things are getting lively. The girls are smiling as they steal long, thin cigarettes from their dates' fingers. The seamen are thumping their hands and feet merrily and impatiently. One of them hollers for the sailor at the bar—Pete's his name—to hurry up.

"Walk me back, could you?" she says to Noonan. She wants to rest, and she wants him to rest, safely apart from these girls.

"I'm going to talk to the fellas. I want to get a confirmation on Howland. I'd take the word of a sailor who's been there over our maps any day."

Silently, A.E. disagrees. She would trust an official government document before a rowdy sailor, and her own gut before both.

"The more ammunition you get, the better," she says aloud. "It's late, though. We need sleep as much as anything."

"If you want to go to your room, go to your room."

"Fred...."

"Okay, I tell you what: why don't you wait for me? I'll say my goodbyes, get a quick reading from these fellas, and then we can take a stroll. Do us both good to walk around for a few minutes. Clear our heads."

"That's not necessary. I don't mean to…"

"Stop," he says, slapping his hand down on the bar. There's an edge to his voice she's heard only a couple of times. "Just give me a minute. That's what I need."

"Fine," she agrees. "I'll be waiting outside."

The problem is he doesn't come out, not after one minute, or five, or twenty. She's steaming mad, but if she walks back down those steps, back into that dim, chock-a-block room, she'll look exactly the way she feels: bossy, powerless, a shrew, a nag. Then again, she reasons with herself, she doesn't know these sailors. She'll never see them again, and Calliope's in no condition to make intelligent observations. Obviously, what she's most concerned about is Fred's judgment. She's furious with herself for caring. Not since she was a little girl with her father has she been so invested in a man's opinion. And not since her father has she so studiously scrutinized the character and content of a man's socializing. Certainly she's never monitored G.P.'s comings and goings so compulsively.

Her partnership with Fred, though, is of course different than her partnership with G.P. Marooned together in a vessel hovering at the far edge of the world, she and the navigator are wholly dependent on each other in principle and in practice. If one fails to trust the other, the results could well be deadly. She and Fred have a duty to protect each other. They have an allegiance, but it does not always feel natural. It seems, to A.E., artificially conceived, as if she and the navigator were the only two participants in a bizarre research experiment on human intimacy.

What they do not have is love. And thank goodness for that. She is too old for the demands of love, which is a younger person's sport, consuming and addictive. She remembers when she first fell in love. It was when she took flying lessons. Eons seemed to pass before her instructor, Neta Snook, finally gave her the okay to go solo. And then, alone in the air, she felt it instantly: yearning and rapture in perfect balance. When she thought of the sky then, and even now, her mind was magnanimous, her capacity to feel, generous and true. Boundaries were merely suggestions. The clouds parted, and beauty was all. What she feels for Noonan has none of this magic. With him, the larger her stake, the smaller she feels.

A half hour has passed. She no longer feels a nearly uncontrollable urge to storm down the stairs. She wishes that he would turn in and lay off the liquor, but she recognizes, under the fog of scotch, that she's not his mother or his wife. She's his boss, and he's off the clock. There's nothing she can do if he wants to wedge himself between those two girls, and smile like the cat who ate the canary. Two canaries.

She takes a deep breath and returns to her room. It's so late she refuses to look at her watch as she takes it off. She undresses and puts on a night dress. She brushes her teeth, touches the little bald patch sourly, and rinses her mouth out directly under the tap, her lips slurping the steady trickle.

"Fiddlesticks!" she says aloud, remembering she's not supposed to drink the water. Dysentery, hookworm, her stomach doesn't need another problem. Well, no use in worrying: the damage is done. She opens the windows and listens for a minute to the waves breaking on the shore. The breeze is gentle off the water. Good, the bugs shouldn't be bad. Just in case, she drapes a mosquito net over the canopy bed.

For a long time she can't sleep. She just wrestles with the sheet, twisting it into soggy hanks. She thinks of taking half of a sleeping pill, but opts not to. She doesn't want to chance being groggy for the flight in the morning.

After what seems like an eternity, she dozes. She has not yet entered deep sleep when the crash sends her bolt upright, hands clammy, head ringing. The noise, from the neighboring room, Fred's room, is loud as a clap of thunder. It's followed by riotous laughing. She feels relieved when she realizes it's just one voice: Fred's. The fool probably got tangled in his mosquito net.

Rather to her own surprise, she gets out of bed, wraps herself in the damp sheet, and knocks sternly on his door. She doesn't wait for him to answer before opening it.

"Who is that? Amelia?"

"Shame on you. You're waking everyone."

"Aw, why are you sore at me? Where'd you go? I came out and you weren't there." His voice sounds hoarse and garbled.

"Then you must be as blind as you are slow."

In her whole life, she's never been this caustic. Perhaps she really is in a madcap research experiment. Why else would she be saying such crazy things?

"I don't think you should come tomorrow," she says.

"You're going to fly the whole of the South Pacific alone? And what will I do—stay here and comb for seashells?"

"What you do is your own business."

"I don't know what's going on with you. Something is off. Your nerves are frayed."

"Why is it that men always talk about women's nerves when it's really their egos that need tending?"

"Listen, if it will make you feel better, I got some new dirt from those sailors. They confirmed what I was thinking: Howland is seven miles southeast of where the charts say. We're in better shape now. We'll make it."

"I was never worried about making it."

"Well...I was."

"If that was supposed to fill me with faith in your navigational abilities, it didn't."

"Now why did you have to go and say that? I thought we were having a nice conversation."

"You call this a nice conversation?"

"I don't know, Amelia, why you're always angry with me."

"Don't you, though?"

She looks back at the door she's shut behind her. Any moment now the manager will rap on it, warning Fred to pack his things and find somewhere else to spend the night.

"I'm going back to my room," she says.

"Don't go, come on...hey, I never heard the recon report."

In the darkness she watches the change in his silhouette as he sits up. His overture, if indeed it is an overture, is insultingly amateurish.

"You're drunk."

He chuckles. "You always think that. It's your fallback excuse."

Rather out of spite, she drops the sheet from around her body, tugs at the hem of her nightdress, and strides over to his bed. She lifts a corner of the mosquito net and crawls in beside him. He's lying on his back again, and she nestles into his side, into the warm nook of his underarm. He smells unbathed, feral, the opposite of G.P., who could live in a bathtub.

Tentatively, she puts one arm around him, holding him loosely at first, then more confidently. She expects him to embrace her, but he doesn't. He's completely still, maddeningly passive. She listens to his breathing, for the rhythmic pauses of sleep. If he's still awake, which she believes he is, she cannot understand, why, if she has acquiesced to share his bed, he is not kissing her.

She knows she should leave. In all, tonight, she'd had about three winks of sleep. It would be incredibly foolish to attempt an enormously challenging leg in only a few hours. She has none of the single-mindedness or the focus she normally feels before take-off. She's conflicted, drowsy, cross, and sulky most of all. Raising herself up, she pulls herself on top of him, straddling him with her legs and kissing him squarely on the mouth. She pulls off her nightdress, revealing her breasts, the size of small peaches, and nipples that are faint, lightly veined, and aggressively erect.

Now he'll have to make a choice—one way or the other, no more dilly-dallying. She reaches underneath the sheet and into his drawers. He is not quite flaccid and not quite rigid. As she fondles and coaxes his, his arms close around her, at last, holding her very still and very tight. She's happy to be embraced this way: rather too hard, so her breath catches in her ribcage. Seconds later, he rolls her back to where she was, at his side, and his arms go limp. He's inert again on his back. His breathing remains steady and uninterrupted. After a jolt of disbelief, she thinks, of course he'll change his mind. Of course he'll try and seduce her. Why, their sweaty skin is literally sticking together, she can hear his heart beating over the waves, she can taste him in her mouth; it would be ludicrous if nothing happened.

She waits. Audaciously, Noonan begins to snore.

It doesn't matter how tired she is, her humiliation is acute, all-consuming, and for several long minutes, incapacitating. It takes great effort for her to leave his bed, to maneuver under the mosquito net again and grab her night dress off the floor. The door to her own room is still ajar. She goes inside and shuts the window. She pulls the netting aside, and crumples into her bed, managing to sleep only when a new day breaks. The light of the sun creeping through the slatted shades feels cleansing somehow. It washes away a little of last night's tarnish, but only a little. She dreams of the pearl. She dreams of her old boyfriend, Sam, of the cuckolded, shamelessly earnest expression he had when she saw him in Boston, after crossing the Atlantic.

When she wakes, with an aching head and a sense of self-loathing, the first thing she does is wire G.P. She tries not to convey any of last night's turbulence or its byproduct: profound embarrassment. She can't bear facing Noonan yet, and is secretly glad when he sleeps away the morning.

Her message to G.P.: "May wait another day for take-off. Having personnel issues."

★ ★ ★

When she sees Fred the following day, he speaks and acts as if nothing has happened. She nods carefully when he says he's still worried about the chronometers.

"Well, you'd better get them looked at again, won't you?"

Her tone is measured, neither abrasive nor unconcerned. Yet if she's calm on the outside, inside she's in tatters. The thought of being alone with Fred is beyond frightening. It's dreadful. Her thoughts run in all kinds of directions as she tries to think of ways to avoid him. Perhaps she can add another person to the voyage, as a buffer. She goes as far as to ask the local radio operator, Balfour, to join them. He thinks she's joking until she assures him otherwise.

Not surprisingly, Balfour turns down the invitation. She doesn't extend it further. Aside from the English couple and Calliope, she doesn't know anyone else. She didn't even get introduced to those Orientals. All she did was gawk at them, same as the men. She wonders, for a female, which is worse: to be ignored, like she was last night, or to be regarded solely as sexual fodder: the one incapacitating, the other contemptuous.

Worn down, her body is now a ready receptacle for emotional anarchy. She can't help but think that if she could just get one good night of regular sleep, a little normalcy, she would recover. She could be airworthy in a matter of days. To have normalcy, however, would require the absence of Fred— an impossibility. He made it quite clear that he's joining her on the flight to Howland. Since she can't evade him, the best she can do is to get the flight over with as soon as possible. Well, first things first. She's got to eat. She manages a little fruit and some chamomile tea. The sardines are out of the question. On top of everything else she's got a hangover.

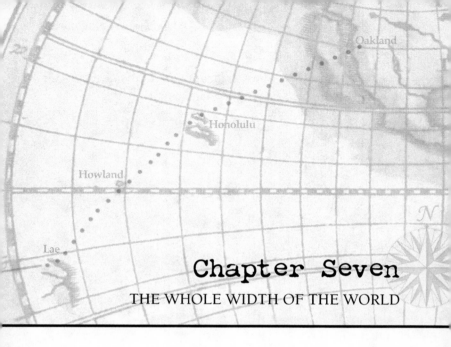

Chapter Seven

THE WHOLE WIDTH OF THE WORLD

HOWLAND. IT WOULD BE HER GREATEST CHALLENGE. IT WOULD be one of Noonan's, as well. He'd found Wake Island, a comparably negligible atoll in the long stretch between Honolulu and Guam. He's crossed the Pacific eighteen times. He knows he *can* get them to Howland. He'd be a fantasist to guarantee it, however. Howland is more of an islet than an island. Only twenty feet above sea level, it's a glorified sandbar, really.

Howland Island's saving grace, in Noonan's mind, is its proximity to another tiny island: Baker. His plan is to aim directly for Howland for most of the journey, then detour south during the last stretch, and fly between the islands. With two land masses within striking distance, he and Earhart will have a much higher chance of getting a visual fix on at least one of them. And with a fix on either, they will make it.

His plan emphasizes safety over economy of distance. It means a minor deviation, and another tax on their already limited fuel reserves, but these are necessary compensations. Being the former chief navigator of Pan Am has taught him nothing if not the preeminence of caution.

He doesn't inform A.E. of his decision to aim between Howland and Baker, worrying that she'll rail against it. He knows he's not exactly in her good graces right now. Besides, he's witnessed firsthand how impatient and pigheaded she can be—their roundabout flight to Dakar proved that. A.E. is nothing like his wife, Mary, who defers to him on everything, including directions. When he thinks of her, he feels smitten. It's still early enough in their marriage for light-headedness and butterflies in the stomach. Still, with Mary, even mundane domestic moments are romantic. Noonan is especially fond of studying his flight charts in the kitchen while Mary is baking. With the smell of strawberry rhubarb pie filling the air, it sometimes occurs to him that the two pastimes, navigating and baking, have something in common: ingredients that must be measured with the utmost care and precision. Whereas his wife deals in sugar and flour and butter, his ingredients are velocity, headwinds, groundspeed, and air density. While Mary has measuring cups, teaspoons, and sifters, he has an unstabilized drift meter, a pelorus mounted at the side window, an altimeter, and an airspeed meter.

He had gathered all data available to him long before he and A.E. started the second round-the-world attempt. There wasn't much on Howland to Lae: the trip had never been attempted before. And so, as Mary bustled around the counter in her apron, sending little puffs of flour into the air as she shaped pie crusts, he did what calculations he could, over and over, making sure the numbers came out exactly the same. They must. Even a minute error would send the Electra veering over a blur of blue, fuel gauge in the red.

Unfortunately, he has to run the numbers anew. Hours before take-off, the Lae mechanics report that there is not enough 100-octane fuel available. A.E. tells them to use the extra barrels onboard. Even these are not sufficient to fuel the plane. There happens to be a sister Electra in the hangar, a coincidental twin to A.E.'s plane. The mechanics siphon the fuel from one plane to put into the other. Fred is angry at this turn of events. He had approximated their optimal altitude based on optimal fuel, not this second-rate stuff, which could be maple syrup, or mud mixed with water, for all he knows. Whatever it is, it will put a greater strain on their engines. And there is another problem: the Electra is fifty percent overloaded. The plane is a fire hazard. More than that, it is about as aerodynamic as a fat lady shot out of a canon.

At sunrise, Fred walks the Lae runway, green with jungle grass, orange with clay. A few hundred feet beyond the end, the ground crumbles under his feet and spills down a steep cliff. Far below, the aquamarine ocean crashes against stone bluffs, the white foam churning, the highest crests sluicing over into craggy tidal pools. No one swims in these waters. The Huon Gulf's undertow is notoriously deadly. Shark fins slice along the surface.

"Fuck," he says aloud, thinking that he misses his wife.

At 9:45 a.m. he and Amelia stand outside the plane, preparing for their 10 a.m. departure. The sun sizzles the air. Amelia is squinting. Since Miami, Fred has noticed how the crow's feet around her eyes have deepened. He has a few years on her, but they look the same age. Fanning herself with one hand, Amelia makes a crack about frying eggs on the wings, and Fred laughs politely, trying not to show how scared he is. He's glad when she opts not to check the Electra's internal temperature. Precision means everything in his field, but in this case, it's better not to know. He and the aviatrix do not look directly at one another. By rebuffing her last night, he wonders if he's made the mistake of his life.

A.E. climbs inside. From a window at the back, he can see some locals and mechanics clapping and waving. They remind him of rodeo clowns.

Fred will say this about Amelia: she doesn't flinch. She advances the engine throttles and unleashes the brake with a certain hand. They're off, fast as they need to go, and picking up speed. At the runway's halfway point, one of the mechanics ignites a smoke bomb. The plane's tail gets off the ground, but there's precious little runway left. The bottom-heavy bird flounders. Fred imagines A.E.'s face is a brilliant study in concentration. She probably walked the runway too, peering over the cliff and watching the great whites stir up the water. He swallows the vomit in his mouth. If they make it, he's gonna need a cardboard carton.

She gets the plane up in the knick of time. They're wholly in the air, past the cliff. The plane complains about its full belly with all kinds of grunts and squeals. Amelia drops low, too low in the navigator's opinion. The silver bottom is but six feet above choppy waters. Fred works up a pint of sweat retracting the landing gear. He notes that A.E.'s increasing air speed is no match for the plane's heavy drag. They continue to hover at six feet. They coast on God's good graces. And then, wondrously, they ascend, a little at first, then a little more. A few minutes later she veers to 073 degrees: the direction of Howland Island. Fred dares to breathe. As she establishes a safe cruising altitude, he forgets how sick he felt only minutes before. He lets go a wild whoop. He yells, "Great job, honey!"

Predictably, she doesn't answer.

★ ★ ★

With the takeoff complete, she's gaining confidence. She lets herself think beyond Howland, to the last leg of the journey: back to Hawaii. At that point, with the end in sight—so brilliant, so promising—she thinks they'll make it. This is the hard part. Her heart's still fluttering like a red cardinal in her chest from the terrifying start. With effort, she wills it to rest. She takes comfort in the fact that, by now, the Lae crew will have sent a message to the Itasca, her primary sea contact.

The Coast Guard ship will know that she and Noonan are on their way.

A 250-foot class cutter, the Itasca has dropped anchor just off Howland. It's a fully manned vessel whose purpose is to guide A.E. to safety, and it has a partner: a Navy tugboat called the Ontario. The latter is stationed midway between Lae and Howland. It will dispense of-the-moment weather conditions and advisories via radio. Eleanor and the President are behind the presence of both ships. They'd insisted, after G.P. told them about this, the most difficult part of A.E.'s journey.

"Anything for Amelia," Eleanor had said.

The aviatrix has agreed to transmit her coordinates every hour at precisely eighteen past. At twenty minutes past, she is to listen to the radio for updates and news from her ground and sea affiliates. Right now, Balfour, in Lae, is her closest lifeline. Faithfully, she chimes in 10:18. She's short and sweet: stating the plane's height and position. Her voice is assured.

"Everything okay. Some cumulous clouds, nothing to worry about."

She tunes in to 6210 kilocycles: what should be the clearest daytime frequency. Nothing. At best, a mumble drenched in static. She turns the knob a little to the right, now to the left. Zilch, still. Twenty minutes after the hour turns into twenty-five and then half-past. She adjusts the controls, searching for signs of life. Though she finds none, she's not particularly worried. Better to rely on yourself, anyway, she's always thought.

At 11:18 and 12:18 she issues more reports, but receives nothing. She's more troubled now. She promised G.P. she would give her coordinates. He made her swear on the Bible, never mind that she doesn't believe in God, generally, or in an afterlife, specifically. She's almost sure, when you die, that's it, poof, over and out. G.P. made her swear, and she did, and now there is no proof that she made good on her promise. She swallows, her throat parched. She sips juice from her canteen. Since takeoff, the headwinds have been stronger than anticipated, and they seem to be getting worse. Pressure against the plane is making the craft shake like an old alcoholic, or maybe it's the dodgy fuel. With so much noise in the craft, she can no longer hear Noonan. They resume use of the bamboo fishing pole for communications.

He writes her a note to undercut a fearsome new crop of clouds. They're fat with rain. The Electra is taking a beating. A.E. dips lower. With all this outmaneuvering, the plane is nowhere near its optimal altitude. It's burning a criminal amount of fuel. In the cockpit, the air's beginning to feel stale as a cheap card parlor. The aviatrix rubs the pink latticework in her eyes and tries to stay sharp. It's hard to believe that this is the thirtieth day of her trip. She's flown twenty-one of the days, clocking as many as thirteen hours at a time.

"Lae to Earhart—do you read? Repeat: Do you read? What are your coordinates?"

The radio has finally come to life. It's Balfour.

"Read you loud and clear!"

The successful radio relay heralds more good news: she and Fred have passed through the storm, and the sky ahead looks welcoming. She takes another sip of juice. The Electra darts in and out of thin clouds, and A.E. thinks, clouds like these don't bother me. They are the same kind she and her sister used to watch as kids. On their backs on the ground, they'd stare at the white wisps, counting crows or just daydreaming. In the winter their eyes would water from the cold. A.E. would get up first, then tug her lethargic sister along. If the snow were new, the girls would make snowmen. They'd tread over to the lake, a good mile away. Just to be daring, A.E. would meander across the frozen surface to the inlet, where the moving water made the ice brittle-thin. She'd see how close she could get to the running water before the ice started to crumble under her boots. When she'd prod Muriel to come join her, Muriel would pretend not to hear and adjust the fleece flaps of her hat over her ears.

Hours later, their cheeks chapped, snowmelt seeping over the tops of their boots and through several pairs of socks, Pidge would beg to go inside and sit by the fire. A.E. never wanted to. Somehow, she'd convince Muriel to stay out just a little longer, to go sledding, A.E.'s favorite thing in the world.

The sisters would fetch their sleds from the shed and with soggy mittens oil up the rails. Sometimes A.E. would tromp up the steep hill at the top of Main Street. Following wearily, Muriel would complain the whole way, but never did she take her eyes off her sister, driven by a pledge of responsibility. Her mother had told her on many occasions: "She is your family and you must take care of her."

At the top of the hill, the sun seemed to beat brighter, as if the girls had summited one of the earth's highest peaks. They held their sleds' ropes tightly. Behind them, the rails trailed perfect parallel lines in virgin white.

On one memorable outing, A.E. took a running start, flopping belly down on the sled. So lithe and light, she coasted on the thin icy crust of the snow, the part the sun had warmed into water before a new cold front had frozen it again. Pidge was alarmed by how fast A.E. was going. She was further alarmed by the horse-drawn wagon that was making its way down the road that bisected Main Street at the bottom of the hill. Muriel screamed for A.E. to stop. Ignoring her at first, A.E. saw suddenly what it was Muriel was yelling about. In her peripheral vision, she glimpsed hooves, blackest of black, with tufts of hair at the back, but she heard no clip-clop sound on the snowy cobblestones, no warning. Suddenly there came a startled whinny; the sharp crack of a whip seemed meant for her as well as the horse. Muriel was crying hysterically; probably the whole town could hear her. Instinctively, A.E. ducked her head. A scrap of a girl, small enough to zoom straight between the horse's legs, smack under its belly, she emerged from the other side out of breath, but triumphant.

Back at home, she decided not to disclose the incident. But Muriel, indignant and tearful, spoke up at once.

"She was sledding like a boy," she brayed to their grandmother. Muriel's complaints did not seem to faze Amelia Otis, however. She was accustomed to, if not tolerant of, feminine theatrics. Her daughter Margaret had spent her youth waltzing about town in a pair of bloomers.

"That's right," Amelia said boldly. Now that the truth had been leaked, she might as well make the best of it. "Belly-slamming, the boys call it."

"She was almost killed!" Muriel insisted.

"But I wasn't."

Grandma Otis, who could not, or did not want to, consider the possibility of her granddaughters in danger, simply asked how the horse had made out.

"Without a scrape," A.E. informed her.

"Well then, no harm done," the old woman replied.

*   *   *

Noonan smiles thinly when he gets a visual fix on Nukumanu Island. The landmark, which is, like Howland, a speck in the South Pacific, means they are on target. The plane has officially made it one third of the way. He takes this in with pride. Having a visual fix on Nukumanu reaffirms his navigational aptitude, at least in his own mind. Unfortunately, not much else about the leg is reassuring. Though lighter now, headwinds continue to strain their fuel reserves. The Electra will need every last drop of its low-grade juice to reach Howland. If anything else goes wrong—a failed engine, prolonged battle with a nasty squall—Noonan thinks they will crash. This is a reasonable deduction, if not a scientific fact. He makes the decision. Steadying his hand, he takes a deep breath, writes a note, and passes it.

"Excess fuel consumption = severely increased risk of premature landing. Recommend abort mission."

She returns her response in under a minute. He thinks, not for the first time, that the aviatrix writes as she flies: flamboyantly, and without much finesse.

"Will continue. Return to Lae too risky. How many minutes = Point of Safe Return?"

Noonan licks his lips and chuckles. Here he is, an internationally recognized flight expert, and what is he doing now? Playing second fiddle to a dame. She's beyond infuriating. He promised himself no drinking on this leg and it's a good thing he jettisoned his flask. It's starting to feel like a major sacrifice now. He aggressively exes out her response and writes:

"Insist on immediate return to L. Over 50% chance premature fuel exhaustion."

This time she makes him wait, which angers him even more. It's not like they have time to dally.

"Believe we can make it. Skies ahead clear."

Fine, no more soft-peddling, he decides. To hell with what happened the other night. He's got to treat her like what she is: a gifted, cocky pilot who might just get them both killed.

"Losing time. This is no pissing contest. Return to L. imperative. Have tailwind on our side."

Noonan sends the note and runs his hand through his hair. He feels the way he did after the torpedo attacks. He remembers well how the boat's beams and plates had bent back from the impact holes like flower petals curling away from a pistil.

All three times the water had come almost apologetically at first. The staggering force of it, moments later, shocks him to this day.

★ ★ ★

Tough talk, these notes from Noonan, but she has made up her mind. The headwinds feel almost mild now, and the plane is cruising at a more agreeable altitude. All her instruments are behaving themselves. To her mind, the risks of returning far outweigh the benefits. How is she to land in Lae? Perhaps Noonan can explain that. In Lae it's already night. There are no lights to illuminate the airfield and the stubby airstrip is surrounded by jungle. It's impossible to circumvent trees when they're growing within inches of one another. Is Noonan suggesting she wait for dawn? That would be ridiculous. To fly all the way back and circle Papau New Guinea until sunrise would take hours above and beyond the time it would take to get to Howland. If the Electra doesn't have enough fuel to move forward, why, it most certainly doesn't have enough to get back. Perhaps he wants her to land on Nukumanu? But it has no airstrip, and its topography is far too hilly.

Even if turning back were a viable option, she knows she won't. Deep inside, she feels a return would be a failure. How disappointed G.P. would be, and Margot, and how disappointed she would be in herself. The Lae take-off was beyond perilous: she doesn't have the heart to repeat it. Thus, a return to Lae might mean calling off the whole stunt, giving up all the progress she's already made. And then how would she be remembered? As the woman who almost made it around the world?

Unacceptable.

As for Noonan, she's annoyed and amused by his choice of "pissing contest." If he wants to abandon propriety in the air, as she has on the ground, so be it. But she doesn't have to return his volley.

She descends to 8000 feet: almost the optimal altitude at this stage. Daylight is fading as the plane continues its eastward journey. Set deep in a cerulean twilight, stars blink bright and promising. She's been looking forward to evening, as much for

174 * CHANDRA PRASAD

the sake of celestial navigation as for the simple beauty of the stars. Celestial navigation is Noonan's forte, and a clear night like this one might bring him around to her way of thinking. She writes back to him, finally.

"Forging ahead—could use your support, Fred."

And then she waits.

* * *

Once Noonan accepts that he has no control, that he has nothing to numb the anger or powerlessness, he is humbled. He doesn't want to cede power—for who wants to do that?— but he reckons he'd better face his predicament like a man. He can't carry on griping. And a physical confrontation with A.E. is out of the question. He won't bully her. If he doesn't make it, he wants to be able to look God in the face, without shame.

He takes out a picture of Mary he keeps in his pocket and looks at it very carefully. With the same pen he uses to write notes to Amelia, he scrawls, "I love you, Mary" on the back, and stows it away. Maybe one day the photo will find its way back her.

He feels utterly alone even though A.E. is only a few feet away. To contend with his isolation, he busies himself with the sextant, the instrument that has given him comfort since his sailing days. Finding the angle, the right line between any two objects: this has always soothed him. If he can find the line, the explicit continuity, at least he has the consolation of order and logic.

His next note to A.E. reads simply, "Do or die."

The Electra is officially past the point of safe return.

* * *

She usually relishes nighttime flight. It's a totally different experience from flying by day: more sublime and romantic.

Alluring company, the moon.

Tonight, though, she is not seduced. She's not at all well, and her condition has deteriorated beyond nausea and discomfort. A fever burns her brow. Her feet feel like blocks of ice. A pain pierces her lower abdomen. Extraordinarily gaunt, her body has little fight left in it.

As the sky gets darker, more black than blue, she's in a tunnel without end. The deeper in, the fewer the stars. The moon conceals itself behind a feathery fan of clouds. The aviatrix nods off. Seconds later, jolted awake by her own panic, she downs the last of the juice. It should keep her eyes open, at least. But it creates a different problem: she's got to urinate, badly. The urge has gone from uncomfortable to unbearable, and she wonders if her bladder is what's causing the pain in her stomach.

Surreptitiously, she thrusts a rag into her underpants and relieves herself in a slow, hot trickle. When she retrieves the soaking rag, she sees blood. Her monthly flow: she didn't think she'd get it. It's hard to believe any area of her anatomy could still be functioning properly.

She discards the rag into the same cardboard carton where she now stows notes from Fred. She recognizes these notes, finally, for what they are: quickly dashed and devoid of affection. She's been a fool to misinterpret them, indeed, to misinterpret Noonan. She remains appalled by her actions in Lae, and still blushes hotly when she thinks about them. Given Noonan's dismissive attitude, she could put the episode behind her. She should. If she could only suppress her embarrassment, maybe she could recover her dignity. But it's hard. She's not been rebuffed like this before. She supposes that the normal thing in such a situation would be to leave things alone, to let the bitterness mellow. Of course this is impossible when she and Noonan are bound by close quarters and the intimate collusion of life and death.

She must communicate with him, and so she will. She will read his notes. But she doesn't have to view things as he does. She's determined to see the distance they've made as progress, not regression. They are more than halfway there. More than halfway to their true prize: land-bound safety. She writes to him to keep his eye out for the Ontario, which they will be flying over momentarily.

He responds, "Eyes are peeled. Suggest you reissue coordinates by radio."

He's right. From the ground, the Ontario must be anxious to spot them, too. It's a small boat, with only a few men. All eyes will be turned toward the sky for visual confirmation. She tries the radio and gets nothing. Too far out for communication with Lae, she's hungry for word from her new cohorts. It's harder and harder to concentrate, the futile buzz of the radio as irritating as chalk squeaking down slate. The pangs in her abdomen persist. If only she could get a little fresh air, even a minute's worth. The stuff in the cockpit has turned positively toxic.

Damn it, the radio knob, it's so useless Amelia wants to tear it out. If Fred weren't there, she'd shriek until her throat were as raw as her nerves. It's unlike her, this enraged panic. Her own limits, so close, frighten her. Normally she can push herself far and fast without glimpsing the brink. But now, suddenly, here it is, and she's got no one to pull her back. Well, no one except for Noonan.

Paul Mantz had warned her she'd be in trouble. Stateside, he'd refused to issue her technical go-ahead for the voyage, so she'd left without it. She hadn't even called him to say goodbye.

Well, she thinks, he'd be even more sore at her if he knew she'd dumped his precious trailing wire. She'd ditched the telegraph code key, too. Neither she nor Noonan were very good at using it, anyway.

In hindsight, she can see her mistakes plainly. Far too cavalierly, she mistook vital equipment for excess weight. The code key, trailing wire, emergency parachutes, inflatable life raft: hardly unnecessary baggage. She's most ashamed at what she's jettisoned when she thinks of what she's kept: three melted Mallomar bars and her friend Gene Vidal's lucky knickers. She's even ditched G.P.'s sky trap and the list of pioneering women she's always held dear.

It's not that she's reckless, not exactly. It's just that she prefers simplicity. Like she tried to explain to Mantz, she's always been a minimalist. It's her nature.

As if to mock her for her bad judgment, a squall comes barreling along. It's large; she won't be able to evade it. It vanquishes the remaining stars, the moon. It all but eliminates her chances of communication with the Ontario. For all she knows she's already flown past it.

* * *

It's no fluke that Noonan was adamant about leaving Lae at exactly 10 a.m. His goal was, and is, to get to a very specific location, 180 degrees and the equator, by sunrise at precisely 6 a.m. If the Electra can be there, the sun will confirm their position beyond a doubt.

He's rapping his knuckles nervously on the tiny table he's been working at for over four weeks. It's nothing but sloppily installed wood scraps bolted to the base of the plane. The pencils and pens that are not behind his ears keep rolling across the surface. Maps are splayed everywhere. He's continually tending to his notes, trying to keep them in orderly piles as the plane starts and rocks as if it's on the Wonder Wheel.

Though he's eager to reach 180 degrees and the equator—Shangri-La, as he's come to think of it—he's also sorry to see daybreak. The sun is a cruel creature in comparison to the stars. Here in the South Pacific, the sun is relentless, throbbing, consuming. It boils the water and corrodes the brain. Fred rubs

a window with a rag. He's been doing this habitually, para-
noidly. He can get rid of tiny smudges and condensation, but
he can erase neither the sun's reflection, nor the convex curve
of the glass, both of which add complexity to his work.

A luminous yellow halo peeps over the horizon. It's time.
6:00 a.m. on the nose. Moment, place, and plane must merge
precisely and harmoniously. Shangri-La can be reached only
by this perfect triad. His eyes are fixed on the window, on the
glow at the edge of the sky. Amelia will be facing the sun differ-
ently: head-on—a brutal way to fly. He holds his breath. He
measures the sunline. He squints at the wave crests. When he
can confirm that they are still on track, he can't believe it. With
hardly any two-way radio communication, the Electra is almost
there. It's a miracle. Howland is roughly two hundred miles
away—not very far at all. He has the same jubilance he experienced when he spotted Nukumanu, only one hundred-fold in
intensity.

He didn't dare to believe they had a chance, before. But
now they do. Now they honest to God do. Two hundred miles:
by air, it's nothing. Now is the time to tell A.E. that they must
detour between Howland and Baker. It is still the safest choice,
the right choice. And there is something else. What convinces
him, in his gut, that they must fly between the islands is the
certainty that the government documents are indeed wrong.
All of his calculations corroborate what the sailors said at the
Lae bar: that Howland is not where the maps state.

He's been mulling how to convince her of this. Of course
she will doubt him. Should he write a couple of lines on a note?
Can the bamboo fishing pole possibly do justice to the importance of this missive? Perhaps he ought to make a rare, official
climb to the front of the plane. Plea in person. But it's louder
than ever inside. He's not convinced shouting in A.E.'s ear is
the best way to proceed. He really has no idea how to appeal
to her.

He's got the awful feeling that no matter what he does, she'll do things her way. To end this jeopardy-plagued leg as fast as possible: that's what any pilot would want. It would seem the logical thing to do, if only they were in a logical situation. They are not.

He decides to say a prayer and send a note. He dashes off the new coordinates as if they are status quo. Maybe she'll follow them, no questions asked. Maybe by keeping quiet, he will save them both.

*　*　*

She's told herself to concentrate, but she can't help it, her mind is wandering terribly. It's as if her id is devouring her ego. Exacerbating matters is the sun, which is turning the sea to molten gold. It singes the air. It burns holes in her discipline. Through the windshield, light scalds her face. Her eyes are not just pink now, but red, and watering profusely. She fishes about for her darkest sunglasses. The cockpit is so compact that she should be able to find anything, quickly, but after fiddling around for several minutes, she can't seem to locate them.

As the sun rises ever higher, a black patch emerges in the center of her vision. Damage to the retinas, probably. She's been flying for over thirteen hours. She's itching to feel land under her feet, to straighten her knees. What she wouldn't give to stretch out in a big white bathtub, like the one with clawed feet in Rye, with a bowl of fresh fruit to nosh on. And a glass of chilled white wine. And a big oatmeal cookie straight from the oven. What she wouldn't give for a pair of worn-in flannel pajamas, men's, thick socks, and two aspirin.

Heaven would be that bath, and then a massage, all the kinks in her shoulders rubbed out. She longs for her old bed, which didn't survive the fire. She'd get out of the bath, dry herself with a big fluffy towel, and scamper straight under the sheets, not bothering even to brush her teeth.

Downstairs G.P. and David would be playing a game of gin rummy. Others would be visiting, all her favorites: Eleanor, Gene Vidal and Jacqueline Odlum. They wouldn't think of disturbing her; they all want her to rest. If she were to crawl down the stairs, they would turn her right around and send her back to bed.

"Don't get up," they'd say, "until you're rested and quite yourself again."

It's such a desirous concept that she nearly swoons.

⋆ ⋆ ⋆

The sun has turned the cockpit into an oven and she dozes again, sweat streaming down her cheeks. She startles herself into attention by scratching a fingernail into the inside skin of her forearm. Just a graze at first and then she scrapes deeper, making the letters A.E. and G.P. Deep blood marks.

G.P. and A.E.: A word about their pet names. How soothing it feels to be known by someone in this fleet, intimate way, like best friends calling each other through strung tin cans. Initials snap on the tongue. They conjure a painful bliss, reminiscent of the quick glint of a switchblade across index fingers, a promise on smeared blood, an oath more solemn and true than anything ever declared past childhood. G.P. + A.E.: top secret code names. Names never to be uttered above a hush. Aliases scrawled in beach sand, scored into the impressionable bark of a beech tree; passed by elaborately folded paper airplane. Perfect, the ring of it: G.P. + A.E. Once. Forever. Cross your heart and hope to die.

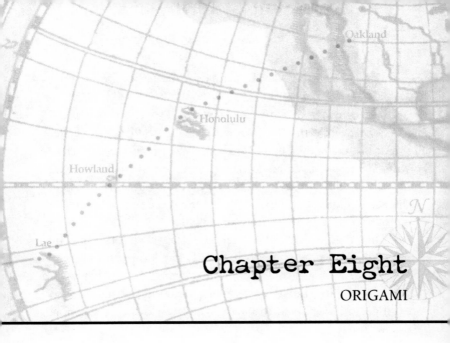

Chapter Eight

ORIGAMI

WHEN NOONAN WRITES HER THAT THEY'RE CLOSE, SHE LAUGHS. It's the first emotion that wells up, not a joyous laughter, or a false one, simply what gurgles up in her throat. Madness, maybe.

Two hundred miles: the home stretch. The last inning. Do or die.

She hasn't gotten a single weather report from the Ontario or Itasca by code or voice. She's sure they're being sent. Mantz was right. Dropping the trailing wire was like chopping off a limb.

Skeptically, if in good faith, she wires the Electra's status regularly. Even if she can't receive the ships, maybe they can receive her. The Itasca, in particular, must have the most contemporary communications equipment. She remembers faintly Mantz said to leave messages of a certain length, so that the Coast Guard would have time to get a fix on her. But how long did he say? Was it five seconds? Ten? She was so often preoccupied during their sessions.

"This is Earhart. Want bearing on 7500 kilocycles on hour. Will whistle in microphone."

Five minutes later, she repeats herself to a blast of static.

Because of the poor air quality, she starts to wheeze. Her throat is closing. She can't speak above a whisper. She tries to whistle sharply, in quick succession. But her whistle is weak, not loud and distinctive like Fred's. When it dawns on her that the noise might sound like the crashing waves or the stutter of a motor, she quits and goes back to talking.

The radio receiver sits under the empty co-pilot's seat. The microphone hangs to her left, beside the side window. The transmitter, smack in front of her forehead, is what she's concerned with, however. Gingerly twisting the main knob during the first part of the flight, she now knocks the whole box with her fist. Hard.

Her fingertips feel numb. She clenches and unclenches her hands rapidly, trying to get her blood pumping. Her finger-nails are blue. Underneath them is the skin she's scraped off her arms. She's beginning to get that dreamy, opiated feeling when the oxygen level is too low.

She says into the microphone: "We must be on you but cannot see you but gas is running low. Been unable to reach you by radio. We are flying at altitude one thousand feet. Only one-half hour gas left, maybe less."

"This is Earhart calling Itasca. Repeat: Earhart calling Itasca. Do you read? We are circling but cannot hear you. Go ahead on 7500. Send word on 7500."

"Earhart. This is Earhart calling Itasca. Need your assistance urgently. Fuel is low."

A note arrives from Noonan and she grabs it. There is still a hole in her vision. The constant strain from glancing at the angled control board to vast sky, and back, under ever-changing light has also weakened her eyes. She takes a long time to read Noonan's notes, though they are short. She's not sure she's reading them correctly, either. It's all too much: stomach sickness, commanding the plane, radioing, and communicating with Noonan at the same time. She goes through his note several times before she realizes it's a repeat of coordinates he already issued. Maybe he's losing his mind too.

For the first time in hours the radio picks up a few erratic words. She tries to understand them, but can't. The voice sounds again, clearer this time.

"Earhart, this is the Itasca. Can you read? Cannot take bearing on…"

The static resumes.

"Damn it!" she cries. She adjusts the knob with the care of a surgeon performing a delicate procedure. When she gets nothing, she slams the transmitter again.

She's struck by a fresh wave of nausea. She leans over the co-pilot's seat and stares into the cardboard carton, which stinks of her urine and blood. She tries to vomit, but dry-heaves instead. Her tongue feels fat and dry in her mouth, a big shriveled worm. The juice is gone, so is the soup. She doesn't trust the canteen of water—can't remember if she boiled it. Afraid she'll faint, she unwraps one of the Mallomar bars and crams the better part of it into her mouth. The sweetness makes her teeth ache, all the way up to her gums. She thinks, at least she'll have something to purge.

They must be closing in on Howland. The fact that she clearly, if momentarily, heard the Itasca is a sign. The island should appear any moment now. The leg is winding down. Yet the sea gives nothing away. It goes on and on, endlessly. Fred reissued the coordinates; he must be confident in their position. Yet she starts to think Howland is not quite so far south. She remembers the maps; she studied them too. Having survived on her flier's instinct this long, she won't second-guess herself. On the fuel gauge, close to empty, the arrow hovers ominously. She veers north.

She dashes a note and turns it around to Noonan, telling him to double-check the coordinates.

With a bandanna she wipes the front window glass. It's picked up a dulling film, as much on the outside as on the inside. She swivels her head, trying to peer through all windows at once. Below her the sea remains unbroken by reef or shoal. She can't resist flying lower. She longs to be closer to earthbound life, to Howland, and if not Howland, then any place that's not covered by water. At a higher elevation she has a panoramic view, but here her eyes are not as tired. She can see the foamy caps, the hypnotically vivid blues of the South Pacific, and lo, even a seabird.

"Pray you're a Howland resident," she tells it.

She knows the island is under her, somewhere. She's practically sitting on it. She thinks she can hear it, through the engine noise: its siren call, bewitching, terrifically frustrating. It's a creature all its own, with not just a voice, but a pulse and heartbeat. It's nothing less than palpable. She drives the plane lower to get closer, although now surveillance is impossible.

Fred is sending notes at frantic pace. She scans them, all the jagged capital letters and underlining and exclamation points, and puts them aside. She could paper a room with all the scraps he's wasting. He's insane if he thinks she'll waver now, so close to the end.

She senses him scuttling behind her, squeezing around the tightly fitted auxiliary fuel tanks separating the cockpit from his work area. He's throwing things out of his way like an angry bear hoisted out of hibernation. She hunches forward, feeling him close in on her.

He'll be mad that she's not listening to him. She never listens to him and he has such good ideas, such important, innovative ideas. But this is no time for a face-off, not when the arrow is dancing on empty. Not when they are seconds away from a landing, surely. A blast of wind sends the plane careening to its side, and she lets it. Fred welters, falling to his knees. He'll be bruised, even more enraged. Her normally acute sense of smell has been all but extinguished by the cockpit fumes, but still she thinks she smells a thin ribbon of whiskey. The old familiar alcoholic's cologne. Is it her imagination or is this whiff proof of a new binge? He's right behind her now, his hand on her shoulder and she turns to see if she can detect the bulge of a bottle in his chest pocket, a flask tucked into the waistband of his dungarees.

She steels herself. He'll try to sweet talk her. They always do. Drunks give good gab, but they don't change, even when they swear they will.

She's jittery at the feel of his hand on her, though she would have welcomed it before, yearned for it even. His face is mossy with stubble, and the hollows under his eyes are morbidly dark. He's a fright, wild and primitive-looking. Stir-crazy, probably. She wonders if his hand will slide from her shoulder to her wrist. Will he try to wrangle the controls from her?

"I'm trying to reason with you, Amelia."

He shouts her name, normally a smooth confluence of vowels, in four distinct parts.

"We're due to stay north, Fred. You know that."

"If you don't turn south, we're not going to make it. You're going to pass Howland altogether. Remember, I talked to those sailors. They know. They told me."

"We have no gas for your detour!" She's yelling as loud as she can, which is not very loud at all.

"Once we pass Howland, I can't get us back. I can't guarantee our position. I can't…."

The rest is a jumble under a new rattling: another fuel tank gone empty.

His grip on her shoulder tightens. She's not going to give, she's not. She's the captain of this ship, and he's crew. Even if he strikes her, she'll fight back, claw him with her fingernails or bite him if she has to. She'll take out the knife from the sheath at her waist, don't think she won't.

There are the hard savage things she contemplates. They thrum through her mind when she should most be concentrating on her radio, on a break in the sweeping ocean. A land mass. Any place large enough to roost.

Through his fingers she can feel him shake with fury, or fear. A droplet of his sweat flies through the air and lands on the back of her hand. Without thinking, she licks it off.

*　*　*

She has said to reporters a million times: in aviation, just when things are starting to go well, you can expect a glitch. And sometimes, when things go wrong, they just keep getting worse.

She and Noonan are now flying through a brand new haze. More clouds, thin gauzy, smoky clouds. She wonders if the Electra is manufacturing them. Maybe one of the engines is dead. Noonan has left her, silently lurching back to his hovel. She waits for a note from him instructing her to go high. Maybe he'll pay another visit. She waits and waits. The horizon stretches on. There's no end to it, surely.

Still no word from Noonan. She decides to maintain landing altitude and hope that the clouds part in time for a peek at Howland, which will appear any moment now. It must. She's circling, doing random spirals through the same hundred square miles of space, looping round and round. Keep treading air, she tells herself. Your luck will hold. The fuel will last. The clouds will open like curtains.

The radio goes dead, utterly, and she realizes, absurdly, that she misses the static. At least it was company. At the same moment, a name pops into her head. Beatrice. Bea. Sassy and sweet, a wonderful name for a little girl. The aviatrix was supposed to have a little girl, but somehow she forgot to along the way. Or maybe she had the girl, and can't remember the birth. She does recall the nurse, the pretty nurse with cherubic blonde curls under her cap, who told her to relax, to breathe, to stop pushing. Your job is done, she'd said.

As for A.E.'s baby girl, Bea, she must be home with G.P., or maybe her mother and Muriel are babysitting.

★ ★ ★

Three times Noonan has faced death. Three times, torpedoed. People think he's ribbing them when he says it, for what are the chances of one man being torpedoed three different times, and living to tell about it? He's not sure if he's the luckiest man alive for having survived the attacks, or the unluckiest for having been exposed to them in the first place. Well, God must have kept him around for a reason. That's how he's always figured it. Maybe God wanted him to see this: one last neon sunset, and what a looker it is: lavender and flamingo pink shot through with topaz, colors he's never seen in quite so staggering a combination.

Well, he was and always will be a Navy man, and like any Navy man knows, metal isn't meant to float. Doesn't matter if it's a boat or a plane. A man can cheat death three times, but four is asking for it. Especially when your captain's a woman. Especially when she's a hard-headed one.

Back before he took off, when he and Mary were in the car accident, he was let off easy. The cops were lenient. The lady in the other car didn't press charges, either. Now he thinks, God was sending him a sign. The crash was merely a prelude to this: a bigger, more spectacular crack-up.

He wishes two things: that he could see Mary again, in the flesh, and that he could lay eyes on the Howland airstrip. No one's even landed on it yet: it's maiden territory. He can barely believe the President of the United States went and built it just for them, in the middle of an ocean ruled by the Japs. Out of W.P.A. dollars, to boot. Shit, he's not going to get even a glimpse of it, not with Amelia flying to Never-Never-Land.

He takes out the photo of Mary again. He lies belly-down on the floor, bending to fit the puny environs, and stares at the picture. He can't help but think about his first wife, too. They got divorced in Mexico. They had some rough times, and a lot of laughs. Sometimes he thinks he didn't give her enough credit, his first wife. She put up with his drinking with the kind of forbearance he's not yet sure if Mary possesses.

He's still got plenty of paper for notes, but he's through sending them. Amelia's not paying a lick of attention. He knows her well enough to know that they're through, done. Cooked. All pilots are stubborn, and she's in a class by herself. He dexterously folds some of the remaining paper into origami birds. For all his drinking, his hands are still steady.

He gets up and totters, hunched at the waist, to his travel bag. He finds the bag of salted peanuts from Africa he's been saving and pops them into his mouth, one by one, sucking off the salt and listening to the last tanks empty. The Electra is down to one, and even that is mostly depleted. Ordinarily he's fastidious about keeping track of exactly how many drops of fuel have been consumed, and how many remain, but as with the notes, he's quit.

He chucks the final peanut into his mouth and grinds it into butter with his teeth. Scanning the ceiling of the Electra, he hopes to see a flask attached by magnet—one he affixed himself, in case of emergency, but then forgot about. Or maybe a charitable mechanic left him a present—it's been known to happen. He combs through his travel bag, taking out each and every item. He checks every pocket, every zippered crevice, even feeling along the bottom. Momentarily, he considers drinking his little bottle of shave lotion.

In the tail there are some random jars and bottles and cans—solvents and engine oil, most likely. He and A.E. were unsure of their usefulness, and so kept them around, just in case. He unscrews the tops and sniffs them: unidentifiable pungent chemical smells, nothing useful to him, right now.

Fred suddenly remembers the first aid box. This is where A.E. found the gauze and tended to his hand. He locates the box excitedly. It's stored away with some food reserves. This is exactly the bonanza he's been searching for: iodine swabs, canisters of rubbing alcohol and witch hazel, adhesive plaster, ammonia inhalants, aspirin and assorted pills, big and small, in different colors, and the golden goose: six morphine syrettes. He whistles.

He's always been a faithful drunk. Sometimes a faithful abstainer, depending on his mood. When he's drinking, he likes whiskey, preferably Jameson, and if no whiskey is available, then beer, the darker the better. Wine is next, red being his strong preference. He has no taste for drinks that are mixed together or filled with ice cubes. He's a smoker, but he seldom takes pills, even aspirin, and is oddly proud of this fact. But desperate times call for desperate measures. And it turns out another adage is true: beggars can't be choosers. He's glad that he and the syrettes have found each other.

He is and always will be a Navy man. He knows all about how ships go down. He knows how quickly metal can be folded, easy, like origami birds. The pressure of water is mighty indeed.

If they survive the landing—and he won't, he's in the stomach of the plane, and thus will be crushed—they'll have twenty minutes, tops. Then the ocean will take them.

The plane's wobbling, there's no way to escape its shaking, even for a second. Missing the vein with the first syrette, he nonetheless injects it into the surrounding flesh. Fine, he'll try another. He's so thin, his veins are bulging, easy to target. He misses on the second try, too. He's being too tender about it. The third needle he plunges in stalwartly, and he makes it, smack into a vein at the crook of his arm. He releases the morphine in one fleet, satisfying push. He looks out the window a last time: still nothing but blue.

It's important that he does the job right. That's something else he's learned: thoroughness. He injects the remaining three syringes into his other arm, two hits, and a miss. Direct, or indirect, at least it's all in.

His body is mellowing already, thank goodness, relaxing, all gooey and easy, even his bones are soft. He curls up on the floor, one of his dirty shirts under his head for a pillow. The plane's listing, and he lists along with it. He's knocked about roughly. His knees and shins are probably black and blue. But he's feeling good now, easy-minded, high, as they say. He's got the photo of his wife. He's got an image of the landing strip in Howland in his head. There are no tracks on it yet, and it's paved in gold.

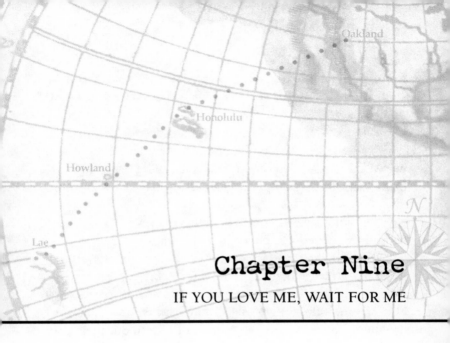

Chapter Nine

IF YOU LOVE ME, WAIT FOR ME

BACK ON THE GROUND EVERYONE IS AWAITING NEWS. IN San Francisco G.P. waits with the Coast Guard, who communicate constantly with the Itasca and the Ontario. The captains of both ships are concerned. There's talk that they've lost her. G.P. assumes she's safe because, in the end, she's always safe. Always a hair's breadth away from disaster, but she gets out of it. As he waits, Gimbels has the audacity to call him right at the Coast Guard station. The manager wants to make sure that the covers were stamped in Lae, per their contract.

"I told you they would be and they are," G.P. says angrily, regretting that he gave out this number. "A gentleman's only as good as his word. Never heard that one? Just shows me who I'm talking to."

He hangs up the phone with a slam.

In Washington, D.C., Eleanor is readying her weekly address, hoping G.P. will telegram her with good news before she has to hand in her notes for editing. He doesn't telegram her by the end of the workday. Her husband's speech-writing team asks for her notes again, and so writes the natural conclusion: "America, thank you for your prayers. My dear friend Amelia Earhart is safe."

At her house, Muriel is putting on lipstick for a radio show. It's a paid appearance to talk about her sister. Her husband, whom she has decided she won't divorce after all, tells her she's being ridiculous, paying so much attention to what she looks like.

"It's radio!" he exclaims. She rolls her eyes and blots, then hands him the red kiss on a handkerchief.

Amy is in the construction-besieged house in North Hollywood. It's a trial run for the arrangement A.E. has been keen on. Amy is with the girl A.E. just hired: Margot. Amy decides she likes Margot well enough—she reminds her a little of her older daughter. Both have the same habit of jutting out their chin obstinately as they talk. Margot even looks like Amelia, a little, in that crazy flying jacket, in the California heat. She keeps saying, "It's all right, Mrs. Earhart. I'm sure everything will be perfectly fine. Mr. Putnam isn't worried in the slightest. And if he's not worried, we oughtn't be."

The more Margot reassures her, the more worried Amy gets. Margot is just a child, naïve as all young girls are. She doesn't understand it's a mother's right to fuss and fret. When the bad news finally comes—A.E. can't be located—Amy will be the first to believe her daughter is dead. This conclusion will give her some relief until she questions her own certainty and embraces a more oily theory: that Amelia has been captured by the Japanese. With terrible obsessiveness, she will, in years to come, read every article on the "Tokyo Rose" theory. Until the end of her life, Amy will cling to the possibility that her daughter had an alias, and derive not a shred of comfort in the possibility that she lived beyond July 1, 1937, albeit in captivity or exile.

The day her iconic boss goes missing, Margot sits primly at

her desk, watching Mrs. Earhart. Usually her hands are busy typing or, of late, writing A.E.'s signature. Just now they are under the desk, where she can finger the real autographed cover she stole before A.E. took off. Secretly she's worried maybe things aren't perfectly fine and all right after all.

The other person with a contraband cover, Elmer Dimity, rehearses the line he plans to deliver when he see Amelia again.

"Looky here—your mail arrived before you did!"

He repeats it a few different times, with emphasis on different words. He decides it sounds funniest with a stress on "you." Days after A.E.'s anticipated landing date, he will suspect he won't get to use the line in any phonetic incarnation. By the end of the 1930s, his disappointment will convert into an absorbing sorrow, bordering on depression. Eventually, he'll retire from the parachute business in part because he wants nothing more to do with the sky. By the 1960s he decides that the cover is just bad luck. He offloads it, with sales to benefit The Amelia Earhart Foundation. In 1991, the auction house Christie's sells the cover a second time: to the tune of $30,000.

Ceci DeRisio never sells her copy. It will get her through the hardest times of her life, just like the silver flying wings, which come several weeks after the stamped cover. The mailing box that contains the wings is addressed to her, in Earhart's own script. The whole of her tenement building will stop by to admire it. At first, Ceci is not even sure she wants to open the parcel: it's so beautiful and mysterious. She holds it a long time. She puts it on the kitchen table and walks all around it, admiring it from every angle. When she finally decides to open it, she slits it very, very carefully. Against the odds the sight of the wings is worth the desecration of the box.

She wears the wings every day of her life from then on, thumbing them gently, keeping them free of tarnish. In turn they act as a shield, buffering her from outside pains. They keep her steady on her path, as she gets married, earns her pilot's license and flying certificate, has a daughter, a son, another daughter, and still keeps flying, teaching her children when they're old enough. When she loses her husband, and then, unbearably, one of her children, she will doubt herself. She will doubt every last shred of her strength, until she remembers that Amelia Earhart thought enough of her to send her the wings, and that, in and of itself, will keep her going.

* * *

When the aviatrix sees a murky patch to the southeast, she thinks they've made it. At last. But if this is Howland, where is the landing strip? And why is the land a lifeless, uniform pewter-gray? Why is it moving? Perhaps she's located the Itasca, yes, that must be it. She's found the ship.

She flies closer, veering straight instead of following the vague looping pattern she's established. Ten miles tick by. She keeps an eye on the ship, waiting for it to take on the familiar definition of a cutter. Strangely, the longer she flies, the more amorphous it appears. She doesn't seem to be making any progress. Maybe it's sailing in the opposite direction, going home. Perhaps The Coast Guard has given up, thinking she and Fred are crashed, dead already.

"Earhart to the Itasca. Repeat: Earhart to the Itasca. Here," she says angrily. "We're right *here*."

She eats the rest of the Mallomar bar without even knowing it. Though the sun has been known to play tricks, she's certain this evasive ship is no mirage, no cruel hallucination.

"I could have sworn this was it," she mutters to Fred. She turns her head to see his reaction, having forgotten that he already left.

She squints and watches the ship's dimensions continue to change. The Itasca seems less distorted now, but rather oddly shaped: ovoid, edgeless. Perhaps it isn't a cutter after all. Could it be the Ontario? Hazily, she remembers that G.P. said something about a third ship being dispatched: the Swan. The Crane? She rubs her forehead trying to remember. Her eyes widen and the ship blurs again. She's chasing a blind spot; that's what it is. No ship, no island. It's the hole in her vision again.

The very last fuel tank surrenders its cargo with a rattle and clank. She stretches her arms to either side. Her fingertips glide down the crowded forest of dials and buttons, switches and gears. There's not an inch of bare space. She knows her cubby by heart. Height: four feet, eight inches. Width: four feet, six. Fair dimensions for a grave.

She's heard it said that in the instant before death, your entire life flashes before you, all the critical moments on a fast-forwarding movie reel. In however much time it takes to draw those last breaths, for the heart to still, you're treated to life's highlights. Amelia has never believed this. She's danced close to death before and never with cinematic accompaniment. Only with fear, and more powerfully, abruptness. She can hardly react, let alone reflect, when the pointer finally rests on empty. She hears her bird emit a terrific squawk and then, with a jump of her heart, she feels it start to fall.

She disengages the autopilot. The rudder pedals go limp under her feet. She works the controls aggressively, but gets a tepid response. She lowers the flaps. The landing gear is still retracted, but that is Fred's job. Even with no fuel, the plane feels bottom-heavy. It's the Electra's big, chock-a-block wheels that pull it down. Pity that Paul Mantz's pontoons are nowhere to be found.

"Get ready, Fred. We're landing, like it or not," she shouts. "Mayday! Mayday!" she says into the dead microphone.

As the ship descends she finds a funny relief in the memory of the Electra's sister plane in the Lae hangar. She thinks, well, she oughtn't feel defeated because she has a back-up vessel. Not to worry, G.P. can scrounge up money and she can try yet again. But how is she supposed to get back to Lae?

The plane is falling much faster than a few short seconds ago. What started as a gradual glide is rapidly turning into a horrible plunge. If the plane noses down too hard, it will implode when it hits the water. She's not sure if the Electra is capable of coasting onto the surface of the South Pacific. It's not as if this has been tested. Still, she must try her best and strive for the right angle of descent. She must strive to raise the nose at just the right moment, neither too quickly nor too late, so that the Electra levels off and skims the water softly.

The engines quit and the world feels blank. She's in a toy plane thrown by a child, destined to land where it will.

As she closes in on the world, the sea looks angry and willful. She tumbles forward with the diving plane, hitting her head on the radio transmitter box. It strikes her on the forehead as if in revenge for her harrying. Her eyes close automatically. She guesses when to nose up, guesses through the pain. She's a fraction of a second late. So intense is the force of impact, the Electra might as well have hit concrete. She's thrown forward again and hurled back, whiplashed as her head collides with the radio transmitter box a second time. The puncture wound deepens.

For a spell she's out cold. Seconds, minutes? It's impossible to know. When she comes to, groggily, she feels blood beading around the cut on her forehead. The pain spindles from the gash, down her nose, along her cheeks, to the back of her head. She tests for feeling in the rest of her body. She bends her fingers, curls her toes. She tilts her head to one side. The pain in her skull becomes crippling. She holds still, suddenly aware of how different the air is: wet and thick and fresh. Breathable.

She thinks she can smell salt. The water's dripping through the edges of the windows and the seams of the Electra's plate skin. Yet she's above the ocean; she can see atop the surface through the crackled windows. There comes a calm she wouldn't have anticipated. The finality of the crash is almost a relief. The worst possible scenario has been realized. She has nothing more to fear. It doesn't occur to her that she should leave the cockpit. The plane is on the water, if not floating exactly, then suspended. If she moves, she will upset its purchase. It doesn't occur to her that there is anything more that she can do.

She holds one hand against her forehead, trying to keep the blood from spilling down her nose. It's possible she has a concussion, or that her skull has been fractured. She's in no position to assess her own physical condition, but after several minutes she remembers Fred. She pulls open the little door connecting cockpit to cabin. Usually it's propped open with a wedge so that they can pass the bamboo pole. The crash must have knocked the wedge out.

Water pours in with a vengeance. She's lucky to get the door shut again, has to muscle it closed with her shoulder and her back, but the illusion of safety's gone. The plane's flooded; she can't help Fred, not if she can't get to him. She pushes open the overhead hatch to a warm sun, scant clouds, a beautiful day in paradise. Her adrenaline, still pumping, gives her the strength her body doesn't have. She hauls herself out, little by little, first her palms on the hot exterior of the plane, then her elbows. Her upper body is out, and slowly, her legs. The pain in her head makes her woozy, and she sits on the top of the plane to rest, hoping everything will stop spinning. When some of her focus returns, she sees that the back half of the Electra is sunk. The regular passenger door, Fred's only way out, is below the waterline.

But for the waves and wind, there's nothing: no wreckage strewn about, no debris, no patches of oil. No evidence at all of the crash, beyond the plane itself. If Fred has made it out, she should see him.

She takes off her shoes and socks, and after a moment, her

trousers, which are soaked and heavy. Cotton: the dead man's fabric, she once heard a sailor say. She slips into the water. She's not much of a swimmer, good enough, a heavy-handed stroke and absolutely no natural buoyancy. She manages to edge around the periphery of her vessel, holding onto the edges of a wing. The salt water seeps into her mouth, up her nose. It burns her arms, where she scraped the initials, and baptizes the wound on her head. Drawing a breath she dips down, surfacing immediately. Her intention was to take a look at the submerged passenger door, but she's sure she'll faint if she tries to swim underwater.

"Fred. Fred." Her voice is whispery-hoarse. She's got no saliva left in her mouth.

Clutching the slippery edge of the wing with her hands, scraping at it with her fingernails when she loses her grip, she doesn't think she'll be able to get to the door.

Even if she manages to, she won't be able to open it if the water pressure hasn't equalized. It's a tall order: swimming inside the plane, finding and rescuing Fred, and in the same valiant stroke, retrieving the things they desperately need, like the life preservers she and Fred decided to store, illogically, optimistically, in a box in the tail. And if somehow she does the impossible, accomplishes all this, what if the door to the Electra closes while she's still onboard? What if, after all, she's doomed to die inside her plane?

She swallows a mouthful of water, although she recalls she shouldn't. It will make her dehydration worse. But what the hell, she swallows another. She blinks long and hard, eyes stinging like mad, and calls Fred's name again. It bounces off the water and goes nowhere.

The plane is discernibly lower than it was the last time she looked. The highest waves splash straight over the top. What tin is still exposed gleams with thousands of droplets of water. Like Amelia, the Electra is thirsty: its pipes are acting as straws, sucking water into the empty fuel tanks, the whole of the body.

Both of the wings are underwater now, she's scrambling to get on top of the nose, the last place to perch. Out of breath, her head feeling oversized and bobbly, she slips over and over. With each try it's a harder struggle. Her legs, unaccustomed to treading water, are leaden with fatigue. She clambers up the sleek wet metal, sliding awkwardly, a hapless scrabbling crab. Her short fingernails snap off. Moppy locks of hair hang into her eyes. Every time she goes to move her head, she remembers that her neck won't allow it.

She's holding onto the nose of the plane with both arms, hugging it the best she can. Her cockpit is going under, but maybe she can reenter and retrieve whatever's in reach: a thermos of water, a compass, a bandanna, most importantly, her compact. There's a little mirror inside. She could hold it up if a search plane happens by, if there's any daylight left.

They will look for her, won't they?

She doesn't have to make a decision regarding reentry. The Electra burps noisily, as if the fuselage is finally gorged, full to the brim with seawater. She's tossed off the nose, with nothing to cling to now, as her silver bird sinks for good. Where the plane used to be, the water funnels violently. She's yanked down in the whirlpool. The undertow drags her full force, ten, fifteen, twenty feet down. She fears it will take her straight to the bottom before it lets up, but it does, finally.

She exhausts the last shred of her stamina swimming to the surface. All of her reserves are spent. She tries to wail, to cry, but is too dried up. Maybe it's for the best: these actions, consummately desperate, are beneath her: beneath the persona she has built for herself. She says a prayer, rationalizing, you don't have to believe in God to be God-fearing, just as you don't have to believe in ghosts to be afraid of the dark. Below her, her plane must be spinning slowly, listlessly, to the center of the earth. Fred may already be there.

Her shirt's come mostly unbuttoned, it's a soggy tattered rag now, but miraculously the pearl is still there. She feels it through the fabric of a pocket. With trembling fingers she tries to hold it between her thumb and index finger. It slips with a plip, gone in the water, and she says to Fred, "I'm sorry." For all of the dramatics in Lae, for leading him here. She's lost a comrade and colleague, one of the best. He's given his life for her to learn something she suspected all along. Flying is her only love. Everything else is infatuation.

She lets her shirt fall away too, into the mouth of the ocean, a hungry mouth foamy and ravenous for anything it's offered. She's lying on her back, kicking her feet, trying to let the water carry her. Let the water do the work of supporting her, if it's willing. If not in the sky, she won't pretend to have any clout. Though cold, she feels safe and cradled, like a newborn. With water in her ears she hears the inside of a seashell. The sky is beautiful overhead, even more beautiful now that she is not beholden to it. How many more minutes are left in the day, she is not sure, knowing only that dusk is here.

She watches the sky. That is all there is: the sky and sinking sun. There's no hint of land, no floating objects to hold or look at. She hasn't the strength to swim, not for miles and miles, and even if she did, what direction would she pick? Is she north or south of Howland? East or west? Is she closer to Baker or impossibly far from both?

She's kicking her feet more slowly, clumsily, and every once in a while she feels them still, feels her whole body still, in the water that gets dark at sundown just like the sky, in the water that seeps into her nostrils, and burns her eyes, and wades up hungrily to her eyebrows, to her hairline, if she lets it. The waves keep lapping over her, so that she has to flail and flap to keep her face up. She thinks she might not bother much longer, she's so exhausted, and here it is: night.

The wound on her forehead hasn't improved. The waves

are washing away the blood so it can't coagulate, can't possibly scab over. Her blood seeps into the water, she's seeping into the water. She thinks, life doesn't flash before you, not exactly, but it sort of fills you a last time. As everything else drains away come people like G.P. and Muriel and her mother, David with his enthusiasm, Fred and Sam Chapman, even people like Neta, the girl who trained her to fly, and of course her beloved father, they sort of fill you, at the end, as your blood runs out, as water and sky converge, one inky blanket covering you, and you open your mouth, and take in what you've been trying to keep out, and you stop feeling the body you're in, the body you've been taking for granted, you stop listening for planes and fog horns and the plaintive sound of your own name. You stop watching for flares, searchlights, the curl of the moon. You stop wanting the stars to come out and keep you company. You stop planning, at the end, as if the hours were plentiful, or numbered, or yours at all. You just, at the end, stop.

∗ ∗ ∗

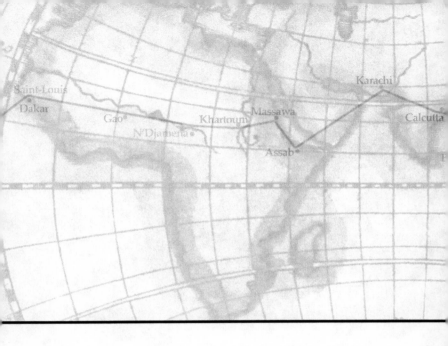

The End

Acknowledgments

Breathe the Sky was checked for technical accuracy by Quentin "Dale" Plumleigh.

Born in 1932, Quentin "Dale" Plumleigh taught himself Morse code when he was twelve and started flying at age fourteen. Initially trained as a radio operator, he has been active in aviation his entire life and spent 20 years in the U.S. Air Force. He served in both the Korean War and Vietnam War. An Amelia Earhart enthusiast, Plumleigh is familiar not only with her legacy, but also with the navigational principles used during her lifetime.

* * *

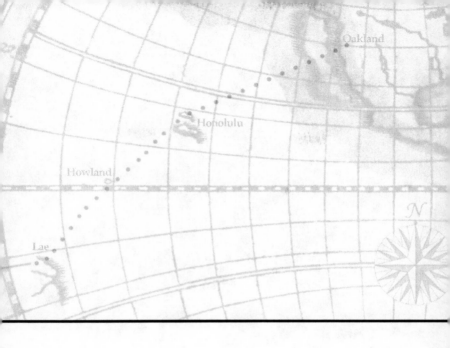

Author's Note

Breathe the Sky is a creative rendering and should be interpreted as neither biography nor historical document. Sources consulted by the author, in no particular order, include the following: *Amelia Earhart: A Biography* by Doris L. Rich; *20 Hrs., 40 Min.: Our Flight in the Friendship* by Amelia Earhart; *Amelia Earhart: The Mystery Solved* by Elgen M. Long and Marie K. Long; *Amelia Earhart's Shoes* by Thomas F. King, Randall S. Jacobson, Karen R. Burns, and Kenton Spading; *With Our Own Eyes: Eyewitnesses to the Final Days of Amelia Earhart* by Mike Campbell with Thomas E. Devine, and *Amelia Earhart: Last Flight* from the journals of Amelia Earhart.

* * *

LaVergne, TN USA
29 March 2010
177482LV00001B/6/P